C.A.

Hunting The Reaper

REAPED · BOOK ONE

Copyright

Cover Design & Formatting by TalkNerdy2me
www.thetalknerdy.com

Dedication

To everyone who read our novella in the
Violent Tendencies Anthology and loved it,
this is for you.

REAPED

Prologue

Selene

"You have two options," I take a step closer into his body, enjoying when it begins to tremble, "you tell me what I want to know, or we play a game."

His eyes widen and his mouth falls open as I slowly pop the buttons on his long-sleeved, plaid shirt with my knife, "a game?"

I stop my descent with the blade and giggle, "did you pick a game?" excitement courses through me, "I love games."

"No, I…" he chokes on a sob as the tip of my knife presses into his skin, "I don't know a Janelle or a Jan."

I feel a bead of sweat begin to slide down the side of my face and I step back with a huff; the Nevada heat is dry. I've been here a month and I still haven't gotten used to it. One good thing about Nevada? So many twisted souls that need to be wiped out. I was meant to come here, and I was meant to clean it in the only way I know how.

"I believe you," I nod and grin when I see him visibly relax.

I found this gem the same way I've found many before him, on the darknet. I put out an ad for a realistic rape fantasy and this is who responded. After one week of investigation, I found out that Earl Jr. here likes to stalk young women and then rape the ones that live alone. If my sister was sold to a sex ring or as a sex slave like so many of Henry Walton's victims were, then I needed to follow the crumbs of perverts, and trust me, they all run in the same circles. I'm getting closer.

I watch as Earl tries to squirm, but he doesn't get too far, not when I have all his limbs tied, spread eagle between two large trees and his pants have been long cut off. You see, I met him at a bar and when I saw him slip a little powder in my drink - he thought he was being slick - I switched glasses when the football game on the screen stole his attention. I guess he doesn't just like to play at rape, he wants the real thing. After that, I could've convinced him his nana was a horse and he would have believed me. He even helped me pull out the ropes from the trunk of my car and didn't say a word as I began to tie him up. Four hours later though, he's sobering up and thank fuck because I am starving.

"Are you going to let me go?" his voice shakes. Little pussy.

"Not just yet," I shake my head and continue to cut open his shirt, "how about you tell me about some of your friends that like the same things?"

He's quick to toss out three names and even where I can find them, awfully helpful this one. I'm partially listening to him throw his pervert friends under the bus as I clean my nails with my knife. I wonder how my guys are doing. No. I give myself a shake and continue to listen to this asshole's confession. Did he say gang rape?

Zander is probably cursing himself for not adding another tracker, Darius and Santos are most likely ready to burn their town down looking for me, and Blaze is probably out for blood. He's going to want to watch me bleed and not in the way that Santos does, more like watching me bleed in the dying way.

"Shut up, Earl." I huff and roll my eyes, "you're giving me a headache."

I throw my blade and it slips through his throat, embedding it to the hilt. He's wide eyed and choking on his blood as I stroll back to stand in front of him. Finally, his eyes lose focus and then all life leaves his body as his greasy head falls forward. I pull out my blade and wipe the blood off onto my trench. Killing rapists and pedophiles is such a fucking messy business.

I rip his shirt further apart and stand transfixed, watching his blood run down his chest and stomach in a steady stream. When the blood flow slows and begins to thicken in the heat, I run my finger along its surface, grinning at the velvety feel. My finger moves of its own accord, drawing the scythe in perfect detail, and then moving beneath it, one word large and prominent.

Reaped.
Earl had to die…

REAPED

HUNTING THE REAPER

Chapter One

Selene

I'm being followed.

Tingles sporadically race up the back of my skull and down to the nape of my neck, but I never react or look around. That's just giving away the fact that I know someone's watching me. It's like those horror movies you watch when the killer is stalking the little female and he's watching her, she's constantly looking around like a flighty little bird.

That bitch ain't me, honey.

I'm fucking excited and I'm hoping I can lead them down a darkened path, only to slice their throat open. I've gathered enough enemies and narrowing down who it might be, would be difficult, so I'll wait until they grow a pair to approach me. Until then, I hope they enjoy the show I'm about to give them.

Earl was nice enough to guide me to a few of his friends and I now have a date with a man named Mr. Haynes. Mr. Haynes gives me the same vibe as Mr. Walton did and that makes me even more excited. I feel like I'm finally getting somewhere, and I'll soon learn what transpired with Jan. I'm patient when the time calls for it and right now, I have patience in abundance.

"Ain't it dark wrapped up in that tarp, Earl?" I sing, *The Chicks* could honestly tell the future.

I've sharpened my blade and put it away in its custom-made holster strapped around my waist, then I tie up my trench. There are those pesky tingles again, making me giggle, and anticipation glides over my skin. I love being the apple of someone's eye and I love carving out those fucking eyes when they piss me off. They always do.

I think of the four men who haven't pissed me off to that point yet and quickly bury it down, I can't lose focus. No one is as important as my sister, she's the whole reason why I started this, and if there's even the slightest chance I can save her, I won't falter. No matter how much I miss the burn of Darius' rope and the sting of Santos' blade.

Stop Selene. I chastise myself, thinking of them will do nothing to help me with what I need to accomplish. These are foreign feelings for me and getting close to those guys may have been my biggest mistake, especially if they've fucked with my concentration.

I pull my long, thick blonde hair into a high pony and check my face in the mirror. I'm going for the young look tonight because any man that prefers the prefix Mister and nails prostitutes is usually looking to hit the young ones. It's an assumption, but it's one that's never been wrong, and I have done this… often. I'm wearing a dress with a plunging neckline, the hem sitting at mid-thigh, and my signature thigh-high boots, but I have it all wrapped tightly under my trench. Prefix Misters usually like their women proper in the streets but sluts in the sheets. Another assumption I've never gotten wrong.

I'm hoping that I won't need to fuck Mr. Haynes tonight because I haven't had anyone since Blaze. I close my eyes when the memory of him and I fucking in Henry's blood assaults my vision and I let out a small whimper. The way he fucked me and looked at me with reverence in his eyes, he called me a warrior. I let out a shaky breath and try to clear my mind, even Grumpy needs to take a backseat. I hate that we only had that one single moment and then I disappeared, I wanted more. *I want more.*

I shake off the lingering thoughts of my dark, brooding guy with the angry scar on his face and bring myself back to the present, it's time to face the task at hand. My new phone vibrates in my pocket and a grin crawls across my face, this one's also punctual like all prefix Misters. I open the old-style flip phone - that's all I need as a burner - and drop my voice a few octaves, letting the huskiness come through.

"Right on time."

"Hello miss Selene," he rasps. "I gather you are ready?"

"Of course, Mr. Haynes."

I can practically hear him purr at my use of 'Mister'. "Be outside the coffee shop in five minutes." He hangs up before I can answer, and I breathe out my frustration. I can already imagine his skin covered in drying blood and my scythe carved through it.

I press my blood red lips together and pucker them in my reflection, my favorite fucking color. Then I'm out the door of my tiny new apartment and on the street, walking to the coffee shop where I met Mr. Haynes earlier today. His schedule was harder to track down because he wasn't someone who kept it routine. But I did notice him liking this coffee shop a little too much, especially the few waitresses inside. So, I staked it out - naturally - until he finally showed up today.

I chuckle to myself at the memory as I walk down the street. He was coming out of his car, and I hurried to rush outside, knocking into him. My coffee hit his chest and the anger in his eyes almost awakened mine, until he gave me a slow perusal. It's always the same, a pair of hot tits, and long legs have their charm; I had him eating out of my hand in record time. When he offered to drop me off at work, I told him I don't start until well into the night hours, and at no particular spot. He caught on and his eyes shone with excitement. Hook, line, and sinker motherfucker.

I stand outside of the coffee shop, its interior lights off, and the closed sign hanging in the door. I check my reflection in the darkened windows and feel those tendrils of watching eyes skim along the back of my neck. They're here and they're watching me, I try to check out the street behind me in the reflection, but there's nothing. I like that. It means they're good at what they do and it only amps up my excitement more, hopefully I give them an eyeful tonight.

A sleek black Lincoln Town Car pulls up behind me and I turn slowly, dropping my eyes to the ground, looking meek and shy. You can't let men like Mr. Walton and Mr. Haynes see the intelligence in a woman's eyes, their small balls will curl up into their bellies, and they'll avoid you like the plague. They'll even go as far as to ensure you stay away from their wives and daughters too because that intelligent affliction just might be contagious.

I slowly walk to the car and a driver jumps out, rounding the tail end. He opens the back door for me, and I give a little giggle, acting like my brain is made of stuffing. I slide inside and come face to face with Haynes himself. He's not attractive - at all - and I flutter my eyelashes to stop my eyes from rolling, he's in a velvet robe. Did the fucker really not want to get dressed?

"You look divine." He leans over and grasps a lock of my hair between his fingers, "you smell like a meadow of wildflowers."

I want to smell like your fucking blood, you cunt. "It's a new perfume," I give him a small smile. "I'm glad you like it."

"Now Selene," he leans back in his seat and his robe starts to fall open. *Here we go.* "What exactly must we do to create this fortunate coupling?" The fuck is he trying to say?

"I need your signature… in blood." It's out of my mouth before I can stop it and I curse my intelligent affliction. I giggle into my hand, and he smiles, shaking his head as if I were a silly toddler. Probably exactly his type, really. "You tell me what you would like, and I'll give you the price."

"I want your mouth on my cock and then your pussy milking me dry." Well, straight to the point.

"Fifteen hundred dollars." His eyes widen at the number, and I curse myself for not doubling it, his chest hair alone could act as a sweater.

"That's quite a large number for a young prostitute." Hook.

"I started young; I have experience." Line.

Come on you furry ape, take the fucking bait.

"How young?" his smile grows sinister. Sinker.

"Twelve." I whisper like it's a secret meant for only the two of us, "I never turned back."

"Deal." He throws open the robe and shows me his cock. If I thought his chest was bad, his cock looks like it's wearing a pair of furry earmuffs. I can't help but think I will die of suffocation, and I'll never see my guys again.

"Look at all this," I coo. He thinks I'm praising his cock when I'm really trying to figure out how to Hoover without dying of pube inhalation.

I kneel onto the seat and bend forward, grabbing his cock. I push downward, trying to get the pubic hair to obey, and place my mouth on the tip. One lick. That's all it takes. Just one lick and the fucker's cum hits my lips and chin. Easy work really, I can't complain.

"Mmm." I say as I scoop it off and wipe it into his fluffy cock's mane.

"Sorry about that," he grins as I sit up, still wiping remnants of him off my chin, "would you care to come by my humble abode for the finale?"

This guy is further off his rocker than I am and that means he's practically under it. "Oh yes, please." I nod my head furiously, watching as his flaccid dick gets swallowed up by his pubic hair, and I swallow down the urge to heave.

The car pulls away from the curb and I remember there's another person in the front seat. I look up into the rear-view mirror and see he has his mouth turned up into a grin, probably finding this whole thing fucking amusing. Well, I'm glad someone is.

His 'humble abode' is a fucking castle. No, seriously, he built himself a castle and told me he likes to speak like royalty, expecting his *subjects* to treat him as such. I'll fucking admit it, I want to be Queen. His house staff bow to him as he walks by, and his maids hurry ahead to prepare the 'bed chamber'.

He has paintings of himself everywhere, much like Henry, but oh so fucking different. Where Henry Walton liked self-portraits showing his body, Haynes liked his to show his crown and scepter, I'm not kidding. I want a painting, but of me, obviously.

I follow him and his train of maids upstairs and we enter a large room. There's a bed that must be bigger than a king size and a fireplace, then more portraits.

"Do you like it?" he asks me, watching my face closely.

"Fuck yes." I breathe and I'm not even lying. I'm trying to figure out if I'd be able to Dyson his cock for the rest of my life, just to be Queen.

His face brightens and his smile becomes reminiscent of the Cheshire Cat, "let's begin." He drops his robe and I watch as his cock slowly pushes through the maze of fur. I drop my trench and startle when a young woman appears out of nowhere. She looks maybe eighteen at most and she's pretty. Her hair is a sleek chestnut brown, and her skin is like rich terra cotta, reminding me of Santos. She picks up my trench and goes back into the shadowed corner, still watching. I kind of like an audience. "That's an interesting belt," he points to my sheath.

It does resemble a belt with the knife handle looking like the buckle. "Thank you," I smile and give him a shy look, "should we lie down?"

He hurries to the bed and climbs on, crawling up on all fours. I bite down on my tongue to hold in the gasp when I see his ass looking like a Chewbacca. How the fuck do I end up in these situations? I really wish I could tell Santos all about it because he would appreciate this the most. Haynes flops onto his back on the bed and waits for me to join him, licking his lips with excitement. *This one's for you, Jan.*

I crawl up his body and I'm astonished at the hair on this man, it really is amazing. Like a Neanderthal or something. I straddle his waist and lean down over him, grinding into his cock.

"Oh yes," he begins to tremble, "put me inside you."

"In a minute," I tease and sit up, rolling my hips forward. "You have really pretty maids." I look over my shoulder to the corner.

"Would you like her to join?" he asks.

"Do they do that? Is that why they're here?" I fall forward and press my mouth to his ear, "are they sex slaves?"

"They're whatever I want them to be." He answers smugly, "that's what I paid for."

Paid for. I really am on the right track. I lean back up and continue to grind down on him, listening to his grunts of pleasure. "I like them and all, but I want it to be just you and me. Is that okay?" I lower my lashes.

"Out!" He screams through the room, and I startle, watching three girls scurry past.

I pull my dress up around my waist, making sure he's watching, and pull my panties to the side. I glide along his dick, not at all wet, and trying not to giggle when his powder puff tickles my lady bits.

"If I wanted a sex... ah... maid," I grab his chin and force his eyes back to mine, "how could I find one?"

"I know a guy," he throws me his skeevy grin, "I can take you to meet him."

"Oh! Really?" I clasp my hands and squeal, "what's his name?"

I have two more names on my list and I'm hoping this sex slave seller is one of them. Haynes gives me a weird look and I bite into my lip, trying to look coy. I don't want him catching on to me so fast. I drag my fingers down my tongue and reach between us to grasp his cock, gliding my fist along it.

"Oh!" he moans and tips his head back.

I pump him harder and lean over, licking along his mouth, "name?"

"John Dempster!" he screams as he comes all over my fist.

"Oh no!" I gasp, "did I ruin the finale my King?"

His eyes shine with appreciation at my choice of words and his hands reach up, giving my tits a squeeze, "I think you earned every damn bit of that money, Miss Selene. When can we do this again?"

I roll off him and wipe his cum into his blanket, making an exasperated sigh, "I'm awfully busy."

"How about I give you double what you asked for and see you again tomorrow night?" he rolls off the bed and opens his bedside table, pulling out a large wad of cash. He starts counting out the bills and barely puts a dent in the roll, tossing me three thousand dollars.

I grab the money and tuck it into my bra, making a big show of squeezing them. He comes to stand in front of me and looks down into my face. Fuck, he really is hairy. It's going to feel like I'm putting down a dog, seriously. I wrap a hand around the hilt of my knife and run my finger down his chest.

"I really wish we could do this again, King Haynes," I put a sugar sweet tone in my voice, "but alas, that's simply not meant to be, Milord." This is so much fun, I really am tempted to keep him.

"I beg your pardon?" he looks at me confused.

I pull out the knife and stand, pulling Haynes into a hug. "You're just not my type." I whisper as I sink the knife into the back of his neck. I watch him sink to the floor and wipe my blade off onto the blanket. I slide it back inside the holster and run to that bedside table. I deserve every fucking cent in there after what I just endured with Toto the dog.

I open the drawer and find three giant wads of cash, grabbing them up in my hands. I rush to my trench and drop them inside the pocket, then pull it on over my shoulders. I walk back over to Haynes and crouch over his trembling body, "not yet dead, Sire?" I say in a dodgy English accent. I dip my finger into the blood seeping around his head and begin to draw my scythe on his forehead, it's the only hairless part of him.

I stand and wipe my finger off on his bed, giving him a small curtsy. "Happy dyin', Milord." I turn on my heel and open the bedroom door. I step out and startle when I find the same girl leaning against the wall.

"I wouldn't go in there for a while, he's a sticky mess." I screw up my face and motion to my groin. She snorts and gives me a nod. I start in the same way I came and stop when I hear her voice.

"I heard him say John Dempster."

I look at her over my shoulder and give a quick nod.

"He's the one that sold me to him," she thumbs to the closed bedroom door. "That John man is a lunatic."

"Is he?" my heart hammers with excitement. "What's your name?"

"Cara." Her mouth dips down in the corners, "it's been a while since anyone has called me that though."

"Where are you from?"

"Around," she shrugs.

"Do you have a family to go back to?" I ask her and she looks at me confused.

"They're the ones that sold me to John."

"Listen, I suggest you get the hell out of here," I toss her one of the wads, "he's dead anyway."

Then I carry on to the front door, leaving her gasp behind me. Next up, John Dempster.

Blaze

I watch her get into that same fucking Lincoln Town Car and I bet the same piece of shit from earlier today is in there, too. She's back to her old tactics of fucking dangerous men to find out information about her sister. She wouldn't have had to do that if she had just asked us to help, and we would have because she had every one of us wrapped around her finger.

The car doesn't move for a while, and I fight every urge to walk up to it and shoot aimlessly inside. The possibility of killing Selene is the only thing stopping me, but fuck, that bitch still manages to piss me off. After about ten minutes, the car pulls away from the curb and I trail a couple cars behind it. Nevada is boring and luckily, I get to follow the Little Reaper Incarnate for some entertainment. After watching her string up that other guy and cutting him, it's been dull. Now at least something is happening.

My fingertips drum against the steering wheel and my mind begins to skip, I'm so close to losing myself. I want to grab her every time I see her and drag her home, and it takes a lot to convince myself not to. I know she'll only run again and then she'll truly be lost to us.

They pull onto a dirt road, and I follow them until I see a fucking castle rising up in the distance. Where the fuck are we? I slow down and let the car get out of sight, fearing they'll see the kick up of dust from my tires. After a few minutes, I slowly crawl towards the castle, and stop when I see Selene getting out of the car. She's looking up at the stone structure in awe and I don't blame her, so am I.

I see another dirt road off to my right, I turn down it, and it finally leads me to two wooden structures. I don't see anyone around, and I throw the car into park, getting out to stretch my legs. I hear animal sounds in one of the structures and walk up to the large double doors, opening them slowly. I peer inside and see horses, beautiful dark Arabians by the looks of them. I step in and shut the door, walking from stall to stall, petting the ones that are curious. This guy owns a castle and has horses, he's bat shit crazy. Sounds like a male version of Selene if I'm being honest. Maybe I should buy her a horse for when she comes home. If I don't end up killing her that is.

I step out of the stable and walk along a stone path, passing a fountain with a statue of a man, the water flowing from his penis like piss. This place is fucking weird. The path takes me to the castle, but I end up behind it and I find a garden of exotic looking flowers. I bend to smell a bush of ombre roses when I hear voices coming up ahead. I dive behind the bush and sit still, not moving a muscle.

"John Dempster will be coming by in a week," the man sounds nasally, "we need to make sure the basement is clear."

"How many for the auction this time?" another man asks.

"I think ten, and this time we have some virgins."

"Man," the second man whines, "I love the virgins."

Selene is here because she found something in Henry's ledger about her sister and right now, I am hearing about another piece of shit that deals in skin. I wonder if her sister is here. I wait as they speak some more about John Dempster, and I know he will be Selene's next target. The breadcrumbs she's following are leading her to a den of rabid animals and she's lucky I found her when I did.

When the voices fade, I slowly stand and look around. I run to the stone wall and follow it back around to the front of the castle; the Town Car is still sitting where they left it. I go to push off the wall when I hear the front door open, and Selene's voice rises.

"I need an Uber to this castle place." She's yelling down at the screen of her phone. I roll my eyes and pull up the Uber app on my phone. Ordering one to come here as she punches her fingers into the screen with frustration.

She's so beautifully deranged and she owns her crazy like a fucking armor. I give her a quick scan from head to toe to make sure she's okay. Is that blood on her face? Did she kill the guy? My cock swells rapidly and I think of the one time I had her, in a pool of Henry Walton's blood.

Nothing will ever compare to her screaming my name while covered in blood.

REAPED

Chapter Two

Santos

Red hot anger and confusion burn inside my chest the moment Zander hangs up the phone after Blaze's recent update. His hazel eyes can't hide the fear he's feeling.

Is she screwing those fucking bastards for information again? If she'd asked before she ran off, I would have ripped them out of their houses and tortured the information out of them for her.

Zander's eyeing me with underlining worry from the other couch, but Darius doesn't hesitate to speak his mind from beside me. There's a reason he's my best friend. That fucker can read me like a book, and he gets me.

"San, breathe. She's alright, Blaze will bring her home soon. Look at me," he says calmly, his voice turning firm. "*Look* at me."

I tilt my face towards him, my voice gruff. "He found her, so he should've tossed her in the car and been on his way back by now. What the fuck is he waiting for?"

"Have you *met* Selene? We can't handle her like that to bring her home, we have to entice her with good dick game and the promise of vigilante justice," Darius grins, not calming my mood in the slightest. I push back from the couch to stand, angrily flipping the small coffee table to try and ease my inner turmoil.

I can't figure out how to express what I'm feeling, and that's always a dangerous combination when added to my anger. It's been a long time since I've snapped and lost control, but the guys know how devastating I can be in my destructive path once I start.

"This isn't the time to be fucking funny!" I bark, considering climbing in my car to go and get my girl myself. She belongs under my body, so I'll be sure that's where she ends up.

Darius stands slowly, putting his hands in front of him to show he's not going to crash tackle me to the ground.

"I'm not joking. I want her to come home too, but we have to do it the right way. Letting Blaze track her and bring her home his way is the only way it will work. If we go and force her hand, she'll take off again and won't come back when she's done. She's safe, you heard Blaze," he says slowly, not flinching when I turn to glare at him, flexing my fingers until they crack. "Hit me if it will make you feel better."

It isn't the first time he's offered to take my hits, knowing it's the only way I will feel in control of my body again. I've always done the same for him, too. He braces as I dive at him, slamming my fists into his ribs and abs until he stumbles back onto the couch, not fighting back, simply being my personal punching bag.

His eyes flash to Zander in warning, telling me the other asshole is wanting to stop me. He could try, but no one can stand in my way without ending up under my bloodied fist too. Hit after hit, the anger releasing from my knuckles until he lets out a grunt of discomfort, snapping me out of it when I realize I'm starting to cause real damage. I jerk back from him, seeing the pain in his eyes as he tries to bury it from me.

I let out a loud shout of frustration, stalking through the house and into my room, slamming the door so hard it almost flies off its hinges. I drop to the bed, tossing my pillows aside as I catch a whiff of Selene's perfume. Her scent is lingering everywhere, and it both relieves and angers me at the same time.

My eyes burn as tears threaten, setting me off all over again. I don't cry, that's not my thing. I shove the contents off my bedside table, a growl rising from my throat in annoyance. Nothing is making these feelings go away. I need my little psychopath to come home and soothe my demons before they take root inside me, growing out of control. I hate that I hurt Darius, but he is my only outlet to the misery and rage within.

My door creaks, alerting me that I have company, but I don't need to glance over my shoulder to see who it is. I know it's Darius. No matter what I do to him, he's always there to make sure I'm okay, even if he's not himself.

The door shuts with a quiet click, and soft footsteps reach my ears until they go silent, the mattress behind me dipping right before a hard body presses against my back and a muscular arm wraps around my middle. He doesn't speak, he simply holds me to attempt to put my heart and soul back together. Too bad, I sold my soul to the Devil a long time ago.

"Fuck off," I grumble, but there's no heat in my words, and he knows it. I tense as his lips brush the back of my neck, his warm breath fanning across my skin.

"No. You need me," he claims, shuffling closer if it were possible, then he's shoving a leg between mine. I both love and hate it when he gets like this, because I feel guilty for hitting him, but I also crave the comfort he gives.

"Did I break anything?" I finally ask, relaxing my body as best I can.

"Probably. I got plenty of ribs though, don't worry about it," he answers, making me scowl.

"I can't fucking hurt you to regain control. That's bullshit."

"Why? Better me than you who's hurting. Besides, it's not like you don't let me use you when I'm pissed off," he chuckles, his breath catching slightly as his ribs must be hurting.

"Why is it better that you hurt? Usually when you're mad, we get laid to burn the energy," I say sharply, wishing he'd stop defending my shitty behavior.

"Roll over and I'll blow you then, if you think it will help," he murmurs as his hand trails down my front, but I grab his wrist to stop his movements. I miss Selene, and he must sense my emotions because he moves to roll me onto my back, peering down at me.

"She'll come home, and when she does, we'll make her scream for forgiveness for days on end. Until then, shut it all out. Rein in that anger and hold its leash tight. What you're feeling is normal, stop fighting it."

"Normal? How the fuck is it normal?" I force out through my teeth, letting his wrist go as he spreads his fingers out across my lower stomach.

"You're heartbroken. Nothing unusual. She's not gone forever, she's just not here right now. Focus on that, alright? Our girl's coming home," he promises, staring into my eyes to show me the truth in their blue depths. I nod, closing my eyes for a second to get a grip on myself, then I meet his gaze again.

"I don't like these feelings. They hurt and make me feel weird," I admit, a small smile tugging at his lips.

"It's meant to hurt, it's your heart. We're all feeling the same, we're only hiding it better. I bet Zander is in bed having a cry wank as we speak."

"Can you cry wank me?" I grin lightly, his eyes filling with amusement.

"How is that possible? You're meant to sit in the corner and cry, using your own tears as lube. Don't you know how a cry wank works, idiot?"

"I do. You blow me until you're gagging, then I can use your tears as lube to finish myself off," I answer, my grin widening. I'm a dick, always will be.

We have no issues taking the edge off for each other, so he knows how I like it.

He raises an eyebrow, his fingers trailing lower down my stomach until they slip below the waistband of my pants.

"Get your jeans off then, but you won't need to finish yourself off. I know what I'm doing."

I reach for my button, flicking it open and dragging the zipper down, shoving the material down my legs and kicking them over the edge of the bed. Darius tugs my boxers down enough to grasp my cock in his palm, stroking it a few times until it's rock hard. I never have to guide him, he always knows exactly what I need, even before I do.

He shuffles down the bed, straddling my lower legs and leaning forward to suck the head of my cock between his lips. I groan, absently running my fingers through his light brown hair. Images of Selene flash in my mind, and I squeeze my eyes shut as I pretend it's her blowing me. I must have mumbled her name, because Darius stops to peer up at me, his eyes full of understanding as I meet them with my own.

"Use me. Imagine I'm Selene, fuck my face," he says openly, not giving a shit that I'm not with him in the moment. I nod, dropping my head back and fisting his hair tighter, starting to thrust up into his mouth until he gags.

His fingers bite into my thighs, just like hers would, and I can't hold back as I thrust harder, not caring that my best friend is struggling to breathe. I'm probably bruising his throat, but I don't think of that as I zone out and fuck his face as requested, pouring all my anger, and hurt into it.

The sound of my heavy breathing and his gags are all I hear. It's not until my balls tighten and cum shoots from my dick down his warm throat, that I release my hold and let him breathe properly.

He drops down beside me, coughing a few times as he tries to catch his breath.

"Better?" He pants, always needing approval. Then again, I'm the same.

"Better," I nod, my weary body finally relaxing enough to shut my mind off for a while. He waits for me to roll over and face away from him before he shuffles against my back to resume our previous position, and before long I'm passing the fuck out, dreaming of our Reaper Queen and pretending everything's okay again for a second.

Nighttime is lonely. I've gotten so used to having the guys around me, that I've forgotten what it feels like to sleep alone. I haven't slept well since leaving, and I'm starting to think I won't again.

I pry my tired eyes open, knowing it's too early to be awake, but also knowing my time of rest is over. In my dreams, I was riding Zander's face, my fingers gripped tight into his highlighted pretty boy hair, as the other three watched through hooded eyes. The moment Blaze stalked towards me and fisted my hair, I woke up.

I swing my legs out of bed and make my way to the kitchen, needing coffee. I have a long day ahead of me. I grab my notebook as I sit to drink my coffee, tapping my finger on John's name. The piece of shit is a dead man walking, but I have to take my time with him, needing all the information inside his head.

If anyone knows where my sister is, it will be him, and I have a feeling I'm going to have a lot of fun pulling it out of him. Men like him don't speak willingly, always trying to bury their secrets as deep as possible. Luckily for me, I can be extremely persuasive.

The best thing about slimy pieces of shit like John? Their dicks are more important than anything else, so threatening their manhood is always a good place to start when digging for information.

I drain my coffee, having a quick shower and getting dressed for the day, not wanting to waste any time. I need to stalk John a little and see what I'm working with.

Luck is on my side, because when I stop for lunch hours later, my eyes catch on an article in the newspaper. Turns out, Mr. John Dempster is an upstanding citizen in the area, if the article about him is anything to go by. The picture gives me a clear shot of his face, his friendly smile covering up the slimy bastard behind the mask.

He has made a hefty donation to install a small park for kids to play in, alongside a youth center for troubled teens, probably so he can track down problematic young girls to groom, then he can snatch them. They are opening the park tomorrow, causing me to smirk. Perfect place to discreetly watch him and suss him out.

I flick through the rest of the paper, not finding anything else interesting, but right as I'm about to stand and leave, the man himself strolls through the door and sits at a table close by. He's in an expensive looking suit, a slate grey color and it has a sort of shine to it, like silk.

His hair is slicked back over his head and the dark brown color glistens under the lights. That's a lot of gel. He's tall but not as tall as my guys, and where they're wide, he looks leaner.

I tug my shirt down slightly, making the girls look a little perkier, then I stand and make my way over to his table. No better time than the present, right?

"Excuse me? Mr. Dempster?" I say in a breathy voice, his annoyed gaze clashing with mine before his brown eyes light up with interest at me.

"Yes? Can I help you?" He smiles, not hiding the fact that he's staring at my tits. Men are such disgusting creatures, I swear.

"I saw you in the paper, I think it's admirable how you're wanting to help the youth in the area. I wish there'd been more men like you around when I was a little girl," I coo, twirling a piece of my blonde hair around my finger. His eyes drop down my body before watching my face, a chuckle leaving him.

"You don't look all that old. You look like you're doing okay," he grins, motioning for me to sit in the chair opposite him. "Please, join me."

"I just ate, but I'd love to stay for a coffee. I'm surprised you're here alone. No woman should ever let her man dine alone, especially not one as handsome as you," I beam, sliding into the chair and fluttering my lashes at him. He is eating it up, just like they always do. You'd think they'd be more careful, but they always think with their dicks first, never their fucking brains.

"I don't have a lady in my life, but I'm not dining alone, am I?" he teases.

"You're single? No way! How does an amazing man like yourself stay single? I bet all the women throw themselves at you! What made you want to help the youth?" I ask.

His voice changes slightly, telling me he's full of shit. "I've seen so many young people, generally girls, who have nowhere safe to go. They don't have access to a hot meal or even a hot shower, so I wanted to provide them with that. A lot of them thrive with help, so I'm hoping to increase their employment options as they get older, by assisting them with resumes and even the option to have a tutor after school. I'm even going to offer a counselor to those struggling. What good is money if you can't use it to help people?" He smiles, and it's almost believable.

I'll bet money on the fact that he is using the counselor bit to con girls into shit, preying on them while they're weak and vulnerable.

I bat my lashes, letting out a light giggle. "You're amazing! I saw you're opening the park tomorrow?"

"Yes, it's going to be a wonderful day with lots of people attending. There will be lunch provided so people can enjoy the day while the kids play. Will you be coming?"

His eyes darken as I give him a coy smile, biting my lip slightly. "I'll definitely be coming, sir. What time should I be there?"

"Ten in the morning I'll be there. It finishes at three that afternoon, but you can celebrate with me afterwards, if you wish?" He offers, pulling a business card from his jacket and handing it to me. "If you can't make it and want to talk more about this another time, here's my card. Call me and we can do this again."

I slip the card into my bra, giving him a beaming smile. "Thank you, Mr. Dempster. I'll be in touch. Oh no, is that the time? I really must get going. I'll have to pass on the coffee, but you enjoy your lunch."

"Have a good afternoon, Miss?" He murmurs, question in his gaze.

"My name's Candy. In and out of work hours," I say sweetly, heat flaring in his dark eyes.

There's always a girl named Candy on every street corner and every strip club, so I leave him with that little idea and part ways, heading back towards where I'm staying with a big smile on my face.

Not long now, and I'll be spilling blood.

REAPED

Chapter Three

Selene

The number of young children here makes me feel anxious. This is the biggest trap I have ever witnessed and it's reminding me of a croc with its jaws open, waiting for his prey. There is a large board propped up in the middle of the park with the names of all the group homes present, I've counted twenty-six. Twenty-six group homes and most of them filled to capacity. All of the children are running through the park, and the wolves drool and wait.

There's a refreshment table and another table loaded down with treats. The best way to buy a child's trust is by giving them all the things they crave. Treats, toys, attention, and love. The sad thing is they are too young to realize when they're being groomed. I look around at the adults, seeing mostly men, and a few women. These are the people that are entrusted with these children's safety and yet money really speaks volumes. If there are enough zeroes at the end of a number, then they can be convinced to turn the other cheek and offer those children up as collateral.

This situation hits close to home for me because of what my mother did to my sister. Janelle was beautiful and so fucking smart, with a bright future in front of her. She had a heart many times too big and even though our crackhead mother treated us like dirt, she kept giving her multiple chances to change. When our mother began bringing men to our apartment, she bought a lock for our bedroom door, and made sure no one could get to me. Even when they would stand outside it and I would shake with fear, Jan always made me feel safe.

Until I wasn't.

I was ten years old when we heard our piece of shit mother offer up one of her virginal daughters as payment for crack, and I had my first taste of what a man was like. My screams must've shaken the very walls of that apartment building, but no one came to help me. Jan was getting her own form of punishment when she was forced to watch it. I was the luckier one in the end, most of the men that our mother brought home wanted Jan, and she was happy enough to offer herself as long as I was left alone. I was such a timid and scared child, I would hide in the closet until it was over, and never once thought of killing our bitch mother. The whole situation became our new normal and I slowly saw my sister die inside.

It took years and a lot of saving and hiding money on my sister's part, and we finally had enough to move out. I was fifteen years old and already knew my way around a man, having been subjected to them multiple times since I was ten. Those are the breaks of being young and developed. Men like them young, and they like them supple, not minding anything about consent.

A month after I turned fifteen, Jan had an apartment lined up for us, and we were supposed to move in the next week, but she went missing two days later. At first, I thought she left me there alone and maybe moved to the apartment by herself. So, I went to the building and asked the front desk, they hadn't seen her. I went to her work and asked for her there, they gave me the same answer.

I knew something bad happened to her. I went to the police, and they gave a quick shrug of their shoulders. Jan was twenty-one and they knew our mother well, they were convinced she had had enough and left. But I knew better, she loved me, and she wanted to keep me safe. It was at fifteen years old I learned the police didn't really care about the poor and that even they preferred money. I did my own investigation, and it was scary as fuck.

I would follow my mother's crack dealers back to wherever they came from and question them. I was raped during those interrogations and beaten bloody sometimes, but I never gave up. I soon started taking free self-defense classes at the local community center and I was a natural, a fast learner. It didn't take long for me to become a confident young woman and I went back to those dealers, doling out a beating of my own. Mind you, thinking back on it, these were strung out and starving crackheads, and it was easy enough to overpower them.

I bought a knife with my savings from my part time job and took up knife throwing classes. I excelled even further in that, and knives became an obsession for me. I also found out, the more you hang out with the crackheads, the more information you can get. Those zombie fuckers will tell you anything if you dangle some drugs at them and I learned a lot. I learned that my mother somehow found herself in the back of a Rolls Royce and speaking to a man about her two young daughters,

daughters that she had been pimping for cash. He offered to take them off her hands and wondered what price she'd be willing to take. The bitch said he could only take one and she wanted a heaping one thousand dollars.

That wasn't because she thought her daughter was worthless, no, to my mother that was a lot of fucking money, and her brain cells were far too obliterated from crack. He agreed, willing to wait it out for the second daughter, knowing eventually my mother would need money, and patience was something Henry Walton had in spades. His mistake is not banking on the hatred a child can develop for the people who are supposed to care for them, and how easily they can be swayed. I was swayed by anger and hatred, my mind consumed with my missing sister, and when I found out my mother sold her to a businessman, I threw my knife into her eye.

I watched her scream and die, laughing when she cried for help. I cried the same words for years and no one came for me, so it was fitting that no one came for her. Once the bitch was dead, I took back my knife, and I trashed the whole apartment, making it look like a drug deal gone wrong. I never fucking looked back.

"Candy?"

I look down at the table full of it and turn to look at the man who must be blind if he's standing here looking for it. I come face to face with John and nearly burst out laughing when I realize I told him my name was Candy.

"John." I plaster a large smile on my face, "this is wonderful." I look around the park then back to him. He's wearing another expensive suit and today his hair is less like a helmet, blowing in the hot Nevada breeze.

"The children are all so happy," he watches a pair of girls spin around and fall to the grass laughing, "I honestly believe their innocence can be inhaled."

What the fuck is this cunt talking about? I smile and nod because what the fuck do I say to that bullshit? He wants to inhale a child's innocence. Who the fuck says that?

"Come with me," he holds out his arm. "Let's watch the children enjoy this."

I want to add on 'while they still can' but I keep my mouth shut. I need him eating out of my hand and it won't be as easy as giving him a blowjob or riding his dick. He's smart and he's careful, he's no wannabe king. I need him to believe that I admire him and feed his ego a bit, then I can sink my claws in with a little tumble in the sack.

We watch the children, but I feel that I'm being watched also.

The back of my neck crackles like lightning and I move it from side to side to alleviate the feeling. Whoever's watching me is still a fucking coward and it's only building up the disdain inside me the longer they wait to jump. I'm game either way, a little build up never hurt anybody, and I can't wait until I use their face like a cutting board.

"Candy?" *Oh, fuck me, this name is ridiculous.*

"Sorry." I give John a smile, "I got lost in thought. It must be all the innocence inhaling." I wave my hand around my head.

He chuckles and leads me back to the refreshment table, "would you like some punch?"

I notice that's the only drink not sealed, and I shake my head, "I would love a water." I grab a bottle.

He grabs one too and stares at me while I take a drink, "you're beautiful, Candy. You remind me of someone."

I swallow down the water and look him in the eye, "I think I have one of those faces because I hear that a lot." How the fuck do I look familiar to this prick? I start to get those tingles again and I can't help but be suspicious. Does John have an idea of who I am? I take a deep breath; I'm probably just overreacting.

He looks at his watch and around the park. People are starting to load the children back into vans and small buses and the sun is lowering as evening approaches.

"Dinner?" he smiles at me.

"Sounds great," I nod and follow him to his car. I didn't wear my trench today, but I do have on my belt and if he tries anything, I'll cut his fucking throat.

He drives a BMW, and it looks pricey as fuck, I mean, why wouldn't it be? Dealing in the skin trade is a lucrative business. I sit inside and fold my hands in my lap, fingers brushing the hilt of my knife. He gets in and gives me a large smile.

"Do you like pasta?"

Who the fuck doesn't, you dumb shit?

John Dempster, a well-known philanthropist in Nevada, is sitting at a table with my fucking girl. People here adore him, he has plaques with his name on them around the city, and yet he sells children and teenagers right under their noses. He has a foreign exchange program where he sends budding young boys and girls, giving them international experiences, and it succeeds because they are all orphans or wards of the state. He controls Nevada's growing population of unwanted children and the people congratulate him for it.

Right now, the dumb shit is feeding my girl food from his plate, and Selene is gobbling it up. I know she likes to eat; I've seen the way she moans over bacon, but this is too fucking far. Why hasn't she killed him yet? I didn't think she actually dated any of the others and the sex was only ever a means to an end, so what's happening here? My body vibrates in rage, and I try to remember what Zander begged me on the phone. *Don't hurt our heart, Blaze. Without her, we'll all go back to being dead inside.*

I lower my chin to my chest and breathe in deeply, holding it until my lungs strain. When I release it, I raise my head and watch as Selene takes a sip of wine. She really is beautiful, and I can see her appeal but that's not what I saw in her. I saw a warrior, someone that's been through hell, and made it out with the scars to prove it. I touch the scar on my face. I know it's the truth because I'm the same. Her and I are made up of the cruelty of others and the strength of retribution. It's why I tried for so long to deny her, I knew if I ever gave in it would be explosive, and I would never be able to let her go.

Hence why I'm here watching her giggle at another man. The rage boils but I have it tempered and even though murder is rampant in my mind, I can control it. She's mine and no matter how far she runs, I will always find her. I don't claim ownership of much in life because I know everything can be taken away. I know first-hand how easy it is to have something you cherish ripped from your hands and the difficulty in trying to move on.

My birth parents were killed in a house fire, and I was found a few days later roaming the nearby woods in pajamas, only two years old. The state couldn't locate my next of kin, so I was put in foster care. By the time I was thirteen, I had been in ten foster homes, and I was entering my eleventh, the final home. That makes it sound sweet right? I found my place and with a loving family that sheltered me until I became of age. That's not how it went at all.

I was put in a home with Anne and Tom Banks. They were an elderly couple and they had decided to open their home to children in need. I wasn't the only child they had and when I got there, I knew something was wrong. The children were too quiet and a few of them had that deadened look in their eyes. After a week, the children told me that sometimes a kid will leave and never come back. I was fearful that the Banks were killing them, and I couldn't let it go. I began to investigate, and I found paperwork in Tom's office regarding the sale of children to a Mr. Henry Walton.

That was the day he found me, and he beat me to within an inch of my life, cutting a slice into my face with a machete. Then, he told me he was not only proud of me for surviving but also for finding that information to begin with and that's when my training began. You see, Tom was a retired marine and he used tactics of torture to toughen me up. Waterboarding was an everyday activity and slicing me with knives was a punishment I received whenever I made a noise. In the beginning, I made a lot of noises and that's why my body is riddled with scars, but in the end, I was quiet. I can thank Tom for one thing, he did teach me how to endure pain and block it out whenever I need to.

I run my finger along the tough ridge of my scar at my lip and watch as Selene's eyes roll into the back of her head as she eats a mouthful of pasta. John is staring at her with a gaping mouth, and I would bet a stiff cock. My knuckles whiten as I grip the steering wheel and once again repeat Zander's words to calm myself down.

The pain rips through my chest but I don't make a sound. Tom Banks would be proud, too bad he's rotting in the grave I made for him, and I did have some decency, I made sure his wife was with him, too.

REAPED

Chapter Four

Zander

I want to be angry at Selene for multiple reasons. One, she killed my father. I'm not upset about the bastard dying, but after all the planning, I wasn't the one to bleed the piece of shit out. Two, she left without saying goodbye. I never would have gotten in the way of finding her sister, but I would have liked to know what was going on. She sucks at communication, always has. Finally, I'm angry that I'm not angry at her for all of the above.

Our girl's never going to be a team player, I understand that, but fuck! I miss her. Knowing Blaze has her back is the only thing stopping me from hunting her down myself. I want to help her, I wish she'd let us, but she won't. This is something she wants to do alone.

Santos yells something from the gym, causing my teeth to grind. He's our biggest issue in this whole mess, he's unstable as fuck. I already have to worry about Blaze's mental health, I don't want to be worrying over Santos too.

Luckily, Darius is doing his best at keeping the asshole under control, but I know he'll eventually snap if we're not careful. He's never cared for anyone like this before, so her leaving has destroyed him.

I hope she hurries up and finds answers, because I want her ass home pronto and her cunt sliding up and down my dick. If I have to jerk off much longer, my fucking arm's going to fall off. Nothing's better than Selene's tight body wrapped around mine. Nothing.

Santos stalks into the room, not glancing my way as he snatches a bottle of water from the fridge and chugs it down, water spilling down his chin and sweaty chest in the process. I'm sure as fuck not going to tell him he's making a mess while in this mood.

His muscles are taut, and I can almost hear the monsters in his head whispering to him, begging him to explode and go after what's his. Love can be powerful, and I think that's why a lot of men don't like having women in the higher ranks of gangs and businesses. Women are beautiful, sexy, *and tempting*. They're literally their own personal fucking weapon and can bring even the biggest asshole to his knees.

Selene is proof of that; she holds all the power, and she doesn't even know it.

I'm relieved that we no longer have to run around for Henry, but now I have no idea what to do with myself. Santos leaves the room, apparently going back to beat Darius on the mat again, having more energy to burn. Blaze might be the best trained weapon we have, but Santos is the one no one ever sees coming.

He's crazy, acts like he doesn't give a shit about anything or anyone, so when he focuses on a target to protect his own? Yeah, it's some scary shit.

I sigh, rubbing my temples with my fingers to clear an ache that isn't there, but it's coming. There's no such thing as quiet time in our lives, so we need to wait for something to go wrong like it always does.

One of the guys will snap, Blaze will lose sight of Selene, Selene will find the answers she seeks then not want to come back. Anything can happen.

Well, except the last one, because if I have to drag that woman home by the hair and bang her until I'm all she knows, I fucking will. I'm uneasy about this John guy though, can't lie.

Selene makes a habit of fucking and killing, never getting too personal or close. So why the hell is she trailing after him like a lost puppy? I couldn't believe it when Blaze informed us that she's hanging off the asshole still, acting like his arm candy. I'm surprised I've tolerated him touching her this long.

What if she's finally lost her fucking marbles and actually likes the cunt? If she doesn't hurry the fuck up and kill him, Blaze will rip him apart. That's the funny thing about Blaze, he's either emotionless or so overbearing it's almost concerning.

He always protects us, throwing himself in front of danger without hesitation, but what lengths will he go to for her? I don't think he's even told us he loves us, and we're his family, but that blonde bombshell is embedded in his heart, causing it to tug-o-war between right and wrong.

He's stuck between wanting to let her seek revenge because she's earned that right and dragging her back to do it for her because that's in his nature. He won't risk something happening to her; so, if anything looks dodgy? She'll find out real quick that she hasn't been alone at all.

I bet she tries to stab us, in all honesty, I have a feeling she won't be grateful to see any of our faces any time soon.

I love how stupid men can be. John has practically told me his entire routine while giving me his life story over dinner. Most of it is complete bullshit, but the little details are real. His voice changes a fraction when he lies, and I've picked up that he repeats a lot of things that are bullshit.

His favourite places to go to eat? Real.

His trips to see his dying Aunt? Bullshit.

Most people wouldn't pick up on it, but I can. So, I keep milking it for all it's worth.

"Do you choose to go to the same place to eat regularly, or do you like to change it up with those other places you like? I love that Thai place that's close to the department store," I smile sweetly, batting my lashes and sipping my coffee.

"I go almost every day to the diner for lunch, but I like to change it up for dinner a lot. I try to come here often, because it's the best pasta I've ever come across, but I also really like that pizza place downtown when I want something more casual," he explains, eyeing me as I open my mouth wide to shove a forkful of food in. I bet the fucker eats pizza with a fork and leaves the crust behind.

I finish chewing before replying, tilting my head slightly.

"You go to the diner for lunch every day? You love the food that much?"

He chuckles, sipping his champagne in thought before replying.

"It's the most central place to go, and I like eating where people see me. It proves I like helping the smaller businesses in the area and I don't see myself as any better than the rest of the community. People want one of their own to lead, and one day I hope that will be me."

Why do all the rich fuckers have an agenda for world domination? Every single one of them seems to be into child porn, slavery, and they always think the rest of the world is supposed to kiss their shoes and lick off the dirt.

The only one I'd met that didn't seem to give a shit was Zander. Fuck, I miss him.

"Candy? Are you alright?"

I jolt back to reality, giving John a bright smile.

"Of course! Sorry, I got lost in thought. You'd make a fantastic leader for the community. You care, you have good morals, and you're modest. You want to make this a safe place for people, and I admire the effort you put into everything. We are all lucky to have you. I'll be sure to vote for you if you ever run in any part of the government," I answer, adding as much sugar as possible to my words. Goes to show money doesn't buy everything, because all rich fuckers also need constant praise and approval like children.

"That's lovely of you to say, thank you. I hope others see it the same way as you do. Do you work tomorrow?" he murmurs. He wants me to talk about my fucking work to see if I'm into selling my pussy.

I force a shy smile, glancing away from him. "I was supposed to work tonight, but I took the night off so I could see you."

"Not many places are open around here late at night," he observes, running his gaze over me as I finish eating.

"I don't have set hours. It's a little unconventional, but it pays my bills," I say and lift my shoulder in a half shrug.

"Dancer?"

"Escort," I correct lightly, watching his eyes fill with interest. His foot brushes against mine under the table, and I look up to give him a small smile. "Don't worry, this meal isn't on the clock."

"I feel terrible for keeping you all evening. Are you sure you don't mind spending more time with me tonight?" He asks in a low voice, and I know exactly what he's asking. He wants me on my back, and he's hoping it's free.

Nothing gives a rich dude an ego boost like bagging a free escort. They think it's because they're so powerful and irresistible that we fall over our feet for them. How cute.

"I was hoping you'd want the night to continue after dinner," I giggle, licking my lips and pulling a groan out of him. He snaps his fingers, wanting the cheque. Typical. I wanted fucking desert.

The moment he pays, he's on his feet, offering me his arm to lead me out to his fancy car. He opens the passenger door and motions for me to sit inside.

We don't speak a lot on the drive to his home, the trees passing by as the sun sets behind them. I mentally remind myself not to kill him, I need more information, but my fingers twitch with the familiar sense of chaos. It isn't often I fuck any of the monsters I come across without ending them afterwards. For the first time ever, guilt eats away at me.

It never bothers me to fuck any of them while I know my guys are at home missing me, because I shake it off and put it down to business. Killing them helps too. I have no reason to feel guilty, but it still bothers me that I'm about to climb onto this rich fucker when it should be Santos, or even Blaze.

They have to let me go, and I have to stop fucking thinking about them. I am not made for happy endings.

I'm surprised when we pull up at a two-story house in a quiet suburban area, my eyes trailing over the flower beds and manicured lawn.

As if sensing my confusion, John chuckles and takes my hand the moment he opens my door. "Not what you expected?"

"Not at all, but I think it's lovely," I smile, letting him lead me up the path and into the house. It's a lot fancier on the inside, and staff are running around cleaning as we walk through. It seems the cunt wants to look like an everyday person on the outside but refuses to let go of his over privileged lifestyle on the inside.

"Would you like some champagne?" he offers, but I shake my head.

"No thank you, the one with dinner was plenty. It's really beautiful here," I state, wanting to make it all about him so he'll keep talking about himself. They never realize just how much they give away because their lack of being humble gets in the way.

"Do you like art? I have a lot in the master bedroom." Real smooth, asshole.

"I do! I think there's something else I'd like to see in there too," I giggle, his eyes darkening.

"Is that right?"

"Yes. You want to show me the way?" I ask, biting my lip and taking a step towards him. He leads the way, his legs eating up the distance between the main room and his bedroom, not wasting any time as he shuts the door and grins.

"What did you want to see then?"

"Your cock is a good place to start," I reply in a husky voice, his fingers flying to the button on his black slacks. He kicks them off, moving towards me as he unbuttons his shirt.

"I want you to ride me," he growls, but I tsk and put a finger up to stop him.

"How about you sit on the bed and let me blow you? I've been thinking about it ever since I saw you this morning," I murmur, fighting the urge to roll my eyes as he drops his boxers down his legs and sits on the bed like a good boy.

He's a decent size, and he trims his bush which is a pleasant surprise. I wish he'd had words with Sir Haynes, leader of the tangled suffocation bush. Men always expect us to be properly presentable, but then they refuse to make the effort themselves. Fucking cunts.

I drop to my knees, crawling towards him and licking my lips. "Wow, what a treat! If I'd have known you were hiding that, I wouldn't have made it through your speech at the park!"

He starts to lose his composure slightly, and the moment he fists my hair, I know he's going to let some of the real monster out. He pushes my face down until I gag, a low growl leaving him as he holds me there for a second before yanking me back. The bastard is lucky I don't punch him in the balls while I'm down here.

I relax my jaw, allowing him to guide me how he wants me until he pulls me back in time to come all over my face with zero warning, my eye burns as cum splashes in it before I get the chance to shut them. Motherfucker!

I drop back, panting and needing a minute as I stand and try not to stab him for being a dick.

"May I use your washroom?" I say sweetly, imagining his blood spurting all over the bedding around him.

"Across the hall," he mumbles, not giving me another glance as I excuse myself to clean up. I'll have to wash my fucking make-up off, or it's going to end up running down my fucking face anyway.

I flush my eye out as best as possible, trying to scrub it off with my hands. I find a cloth in the cupboard under the sink which helps get the rest of it off, and by the time I wander back into the bedroom, John's snoring on his back, his soft cock still exposed.

I didn't even have to fuck him, nice.

I call for an uber and leave the house, waiting on the side of the road, the familiar tingle running down my spine as I feel eyes on me. My stalker is good, I'll give them that.

REAPED

HUNTING THE REAPER

Chapter Five

Blaze

Selene leaves his house looking less than sated and I can't help but grin. When I fucked her, she could barely stand afterward, and right now she looks ready to tear into the concrete with her heels. John Dempster either has erectile difficulties or my girl knows who she belongs to. Maybe when she eyes a new dick, she sees one of ours.

I let her leave and don't bother following her back to her tiny ass apartment. I know where to find her anyway; what I really want to do is watch our new friend John. What he doesn't know is that whomever Selene befriends, I do too, and I feel sorry for any motherfucker that I have in my sights. I slouch down in my seat and blow some air on my coffee to cool it down, time to see who visits John when everyone else is in a slumber.

It's a few hours later and I watch as a pickup truck pulls up. It has one of those trailers you attach to the hitch behind it, I see horses transported in those, but I know this time there aren't any fucking horses. Those air holes are to keep the skin suits breathing, because that's all they really are now, an empty shell of what they once were. Something inside me ignites when I realize Selene is braving a dangerous road and if this was her plan all along, I might just kill her.

These aren't the type of people you infiltrate on your own, no matter how trained you are, and they're successful because they can sniff out the rats. No matter how often she uses her pussy and tries to claim that as her business, they will eventually catch on. She's lucky I'm here with her and she'll show me her appreciation for it soon. If I decide to keep her alive for it. I'm fucking pissed at her, and I still don't know if keeping her breathing will be beneficial for us. Look how much she's fucked with Santos and Zander. Zander hides it better, but Santos has gone off the deep end, not that he wasn't straddling it before she showed up.

The license plate on the pickup says Kansas and I huff knowing this is not limited to being just local. These are big time players, and I would go as far to assume bigger than Walton ever was.

John Dempster's house is modest, but I wonder what his basement looks like and just how far it extends. Or maybe he has a shed in the backyard for when his *shipments* arrive, a holding place, and seemingly unobscured. I want nothing more than to sneak onto the property and find out for myself, but the whole place is littered with cameras.

The downfall of Dempster's need to look normal and blend easily is that his house has neighbors, close ones. Both houses beside his have no cameras and I bet if I get into one of their backyards, I'll be able to get a better picture of what's around his house. I wait for the men to exit the pickup truck and when John opens the door to let them in, I quickly get out of the car. I jog up the neighbor's driveway to his right and I hear quiet crying coming from inside the trailer. Just as I thought.

I hop over the small fence leading to the backyard and breathe out a sigh of relief when the fence is only six feet tall. I can see over at my six-and-a-half-foot height. John does indeed have a structure in his backyard made of cinderblocks and I know that's not a typical shed. So, is this what they do, line the people up and walk them inside? That can't be it, and the more I try to look, the more I see that the structure has no fucking door. There's a secret entrance somewhere. I bet it's a tunnel from the basement and I bet that structure is fucking soundproofed. How do the neighbors not question a doorless structure?

I hear noises from the front of the house, so I creep back towards the driveway and crouch down to listen.

"I'll open the garage, but I need this to be quicker than last time." This must be John, "no fucking around."

Two guys answer in a monotone 'yes, boss' and I hear the truck being backed into the garage. Is the entrance to the secret tunnel there?

I want to lift my head and look over the fence, but I don't want to risk getting caught, I still haven't found out enough information. I'd have to kill everyone and that would leave Selene without answers, ensuring she stayed here longer. We are all coming to the end of our patience with her being away and I'm supposed to be helping to speed this mission up, not slow it down. But I do crave a little bloodshed.

I hear hinges creak and metal banging off metal, but I can't decipher what's being opened and closed. I hear children crying softly and every now and then the crack of skin on skin, followed by a whimper. It takes about fifteen minutes and then the night falls back into silence. A few minutes after that, I hear the hinges creak again and the booming of doors shutting in the still of the night. The sound of the truck starting and pulling out of the garage fills the air, the engine loud until it disappears down the road. Without much more to learn, I head back to my car, and watch John's house a little longer, curious about what happens next.

It's a good thing I don't sleep much.

Craving coffee and some of Selene's bacon, I scroll through my phone. I send a quick text to Zander that I have some info, promising to call later, and then hear the motor of the garage door opening. I slouch down and watch as John pulls out of the garage in his BMW, closing it quickly before he speeds down the street. He can't be leaving for too long, considering the company he has, and my stomach burns with jealousy as I imagine him possibly picking up my girl for breakfast.

I look at the dash and snort when it says six a.m. knowing fully well that she's not up yet. I've learned her routine and I know she'll be asleep for at least another two hours, then she's off playing P.I. I settle in, knowing the business as I do, and wait for the buyer to show up today. Nobody wants to sit on product, regardless of what the business is. You're not making money if it's chilling in your possession. One hour later, John returns with another van in tow, and this time when the door opens, I freeze. It can't fucking be, but I know my eyes aren't deceiving me, and I know well enough, because this man has been in my life since I was thirteen. Mack Delaney.

He was Henry Walton's 'mover' meaning he picked up the imports and exported them. He moved skin and he did it for Tom Banks as well. My first run in with Mack was when I was thirteen years old, and I got to watch as he loaded up two of my foster siblings into a van much the same as he's driving now. Motherfucker.

The fat fuck lights up what will be his first of many smokes and laughs with John, his gapped tooth mouth on full display. Is his name on Selene's list as well? My blood runs cold at the thought of her trying to coax information out of him and knowing he enjoys killing women, then fucking their corpses.

No, I can't let her deal with him on her own and that means I will have to step in before that point.

I tried to make plans with John Dweebster today but he's busy apparently. I really don't like the sound of that and it's eating at my brain. I should go by his house and pop in unannounced like a crazy woman, no one would ever disagree with that statement. The only thing stopping me is that I know nothing yet. I'm taking it slow with him, draining him bit by bit, and when I finally confirm the last name on my list, I will fucking gut him.

I look down at my notebook and chew on the end of my pencil. Earl gave me the name Delaney and I know that's a last name. It's common enough and when I searched for it in the Nevada directory, thirty-two options came up. I could go through all thirty-two and cross them out one by one, but even I know this Delaney may be from out of state. I need to work over John some more and make him trust me. I want him to believe since I'm in the sex industry that maybe I have potential to help him out. I only have to nudge him gently. If I push too hard too soon, he'll get spooked.

Since I have all this time on my hands today, I decide to take a tour of the area I'm living in and try to hear what the word is on the street. I know some of the best information is found on street corners or in darkened allies and I am no stranger to either one. I pull on my trench - knowing I will die of the heat - because it's my security blanket and fasten my 'belt' around my waist.

It's nine in the morning, and the sun is already blasting hot, sweat already forming on the back of my neck. I've been through worse and dealing with a little heat is no big deal. I start for the coffee shop I frequent every morning, loving the dark roast and sometimes pairing it with a side of pastry. Sometimes sitting there; you hear things as well. People love gossiping over coffee.

The bell dings as I step in and the girl behind the counter waves, already so accustomed to my morning visits. I smile and head for the counter, smiling wider when she puts my order in front of me.

"I knew you'd be by," she grins and gives me a quick once over.

"Thank you, Wendy." I smile.

I pay her and head to my usual table in the center of the room, watching as the place fills up around me. I sip my coffee and open the paper in front of me, gasping when I see none other than King Haynes himself. His smiling face mocks me as I quickly read the article.

Eugene Haynes was found slain in his home last night and word is one of his house attendants is under suspicion.

House attendant? Do they mean his sex maids? I think back to that girl I found in the hallway and my heart squeezes. I hope she got out. I quickly skim over the rest and find no other useful information, slapping the paper closed in frustration.

"Mr. Haynes was killed in his own home," my ears pick up the conversation behind me. It sounds like two older men, and I also hear the rustle of a newspaper.

"I heard," the other grunts, "he was an odd one, living up there in a damn castle."

"He had all those maids and such," the first carries on, "maybe he was mistreating them."

"I wouldn't doubt it."

I like that narrative floating around because I know he didn't get the traditional form of justice, but at least his name can be sullied, and those girls can claim self-defense. I get up out of my seat, taking my pastry to go, and dumping my now chilled coffee in the trash. I walk out to the sidewalk and look up and down the street.

I know a small farmer's market is to my right and I could probably start there for gossip. Or I could go to the left where the strip of bars is, knowing it's early, and still willing to bet they'll all have patrons. Left it is.

Farmer's Markets are for non-GMO moms and organic food humpers. Not that I disagree with that, I never had the choice when I was growing up, instant anything was my only option. Besides, I know how to converse with drunks better than trophy wives.

My first bar has a few men on the stools, and I find a booth, ordering a greasy breakfast. I love a greasy pub meal. I dig into my dippy eggs and crispy bacon, my moans attracting all sorts of stares, but fuck them, this shit is amazing. A waitress comes by and refills my coffee, chuckling at my appreciative display. I watch the TV and the news channel is running the story on Haynes.

"Did you know him?" I ask the girl, and she shrugs.

"His rich blood was never in here."

"Do you think he was actually killed by his maid?" I ask with a snort.

She gives me a once over and deems me no threat, "there were rumors about him." She whispers.

"Let me guess," I tap my chin, "he danced in the rain naked and sacrificed babies."

She chuckles and shakes her head, "more like those girls he had up there," she looks around, "weren't… you know… employed."

"Really?" I sit up. Bingo. "What else?"

"We've been having a lot of young women going missing here," she clears her throat, "from the night jobs." Prostitution.

"Go on."

"I knew a few of them and they were regulars in here every night, looking for business. Then they stopped showing up."

"Huh." I sit back.

"Are you… um… a night worker?"

"Yes." I reply without hesitation, "so thank you for the heads up."

She nods and continues back to the bar, looking over at me every now and then. Once my breakfast is done, I get up and toss her down a couple hundred dollars. Her info was good, and Haynes is paying for it.

It's six bars later and a throbbing head when I finally get back to my apartment; I write down everything I was told. Most of the information is the same, girls going missing, and relief that Haynes is dead. You're welcome y'all, I grin to myself. But it's the last thing I write that sends chills down my spine.

The number of children reported as runaways from group homes across Nevada is rising, except no one genuinely believes they've run away.

I need to speed up this situation with John and I need to do it soon. I don't want any more children or young women falling prey to him or Delaney.

REAPED

Chapter Six

Selene

Moans fill my ears as I make my way past the dark allies in the middle of the night, the night strip well and truly underway. A lot of the prostitutes do business in dark corners or out in the open, not giving a fuck who sees them.

I am glad my targets always seem to be rich; it means I get to do business in the back of flashy cars with tinted windows, giving me a fraction of privacy. Then again, I'm grateful for the privacy so no one sees me stab them afterwards, not because it hides my naked body. I don't give a shit about that.

I can sense eyes on me, and even though I know people are glancing at me, I know it's my stalker. I thought they would've made themselves known by now, but they haven't even left a hint of their existence, other than the burning sensation on my skin from their eyes.

"How much for a ride, sugar?"

I slow my steps and glance up at the young man who's running his eyes over me with appreciation, relief rolling through me to see he isn't an old shriveled up fossil. I know it's work, but if I have to endure one more limp noodle dicked, old cunt this week, chances are high I'm going to sew my fucking flaps together and call it a day.

I cock my head to the side, giving him a small smile. "That depends on the kind of ride you want. Aren't you a little young and little too pretty to be paying for sex? I doubt you struggle to reel the girls in."

"Aren't you a little too pretty and a little too sweet to be standing out here like a cracked-out whore?" he throws back without hesitation, making me grin.

"Touché. So, what did you want? Need a blowie to put a pep in your step?"

He snorts, stepping closer but not grabbing at me like I anticipated. Apparently, some men aren't complete pigs.

"I can get a blowie anywhere, babe. A decent lay is another thing, though. So, how much does it cost to rock your world?" he asks with a smirk, and I have to bite back a laugh that almost leaves me. They always think they're rocking my world, but in reality, I get a shitty lay and no orgasm, while they're left panting and satisfied.

"Three grand, and it's yours."

"Two and a half," he drawls, earning a laugh that flies from my lips.

"This isn't a fucking auction, asshole. Take it or leave it."

"How about three grand, but if I make you dizzy from a pile of orgasms, it's two and a half?" he barters, his lip lifting into a nasty smirk.

"You talk a lot of game, Mr.?"

"You don't really need my name, do you?" he asks swiftly, telling me the fuckbag is probably engaged or married. He's too nice for his own good.

"Not particularly, my clients usually like me screaming their names, I personally don't give a shit if I know it or not, though. So, where did you want to do this?" I ask, his eyes drifting over towards the brick wall by the dumpster. Lovely.

"No car?" I half joke, his eyes light up in the dark with the reflection of the streetlamp.

"Nope. You one of the fancy girls who are grossed out by fucking outside in the open?" he teases, making me roll my eyes. Why the fuck is this bastard joking around like we're old friends? I should gut him, just to prove I'm in charge here.

I take his hand, tugging him towards the wall and concealing us in the shadows.

"Sue me, I like to be comfortable when I'm working. I have no problem fucking outside though. Drop them," I exclaim, motioning to his pants as if I have somewhere to be. Technically, I'm supposed to be sussing out the corner by the old railroad tracks where one of the recent missing prostitutes had been last seen - so the whispers told me - but I can't exactly turn the guy away. For all I know, this guy could be the freak taking them; I need to get close to anyone who goes out of their way to ask me for business.

I wish the bastard would pick me; he can make my job a hell of a lot easier if he hands himself over on a silver fucking platter.

The guy chuckles, unbuttoning his pants and pushing them down his legs, raising an eyebrow in challenge. "Well? You next, Blondie."

Pet names now? Argh. Yuck. I change my mind, he's a pig too.

I'm only wearing a tight emerald skirt and a lacy shirt that probably has less material than a bra, so I roll the skirt up over my waist and tug my tiny thong down my legs, stepping out of it with a grin.

"So, how do you want to *blow my mind*?" I sass, knowing I'm about to be let down as usual. The moment he pulls his boxers down, I have to hold back a groan of appreciation. There's rarely a time that I admire a cock, but he's clearly blessed. No lie.

He takes my elbow and pushes my front gently into the wall, the cool brick work causing my nipples to pebble against the material.

"Am I on a time limit?" he purrs in my ear, a light laugh leaving me.

"Never needed one. Why? You think you're good enough to be charged hourly? I highly doubt I'll have to give you that kind of rate. Go ahead and surprise me though."

His hand rests on my waist, squeezing slightly as he fists himself with his other hand. He's gliding a condom along his length, and guides it closer to my pussy, teasing me and confusing the hell out of me. Why the fuck is he teasing me?

"Do you have rules?" he asks randomly, making me snap.

"Would you shut the fuck up and fuck me? You're not paying me to talk," I hiss, gasping in surprise as he slaps his cock against my pussy, biting my shoulder firmly but not painfully.

"I don't want to hurt you, *sue me*," he mocks, rubbing himself in my juices before slowly pushing inside.

"You talk too much," I grit out, but I can't hold back the breathy moan that surfaces as he grinds into me at a surprisingly good angle.

"You'll be the one making too much noise in a minute, babe," he practically whispers, holding my waist with both hands and thrusting firmly into me, alternating between grinds and trusts until I feel the familiar tingle.

"No fucking way," I mutter, disbelief coursing through me, this fucker is going to pull a goddamn orgasm from me. They never manage to do that, mainly because they don't give a shit about me feeling good. They pay me to make *them* feel good. Most don't know how to find my g-spot even if I give them a fucking map.

One of his hands leaves my waist and snakes around my front, his fingers lightly but quickly strumming across my clit until my legs shake and my pussy clamps around his cock, a scream leaving my lips in response.

He fucks me harder, his teeth grazing my neck as a growl erupts from him. "Again." For real? This guy is weird as fuck. Does he really want to pay me to make me feel good? I'm not going to say no.

My bare stomach is starting to get chaffed up from the bricks, but the bite of pain is needed to make it not so nice. I don't do nice sex, ever, especially from a client. Zander's face flashes in my mind, and I squeeze my eyes shut and focus on the burn from the bricks, the guy behind me working hard to pull another climax from me.

The second one isn't as powerful as the first, but it still causes my legs to shake, and he absently puts an arm around my middle to stop me from falling on my ass, the sting of the rash on my stomach becomes a welcomed distraction. He's lasted longer than my other clients, but he's also a lot younger than most, so he probably has good stamina trained into him. His lips trail down my neck, and I fight the urge to pull away. I don't want nice.

"I need to come," he grunts, making me snort.

"Then come."

He buries deep and comes, resting his forehead on the back of my head as he catches his breath. I hate that it's nice, which is stupid. I've spent years wishing my clients had some fucking respect, but now that I've found one who treats me properly, guilt swarms inside me for enjoying it.

I imagine Santos' tired chuckle after we finish, and we joke about something. Darius' banter as he jokes with us. Zander's sweet words that wouldn't seem so sweet to anyone else but were exactly what I'd need to hear at the time. Blaze's intense eyes as he watches me come apart.

What I just did is supposed to be work, so why the fuck do I hate myself for it?

The guy steps back, tosses his condom aside, and fixes his pants, surprising me ever more as he bends over to snatch my panties from the ground, leaning down and offering me to put my feet into them. I silently do, and the moment his eyes trail up my body, they latch onto the bloodied scrapes on my stomach.

"Fuck, I hurt you!" he barks before I can shrug him off, his gentle hands grabbing my waist as his thumbs move up and down my hips while he inspects the damage.

"It's fine," I mumble, but he fixes my skirt properly and takes my hand, tugging me down the street. "Where are we going?" I demand, wondering if maybe he is the kidnapping bastard after all, but we stop by a random building as he ushers me closer, pulling the shirt over his head and turning a tap that's attached to the exterior.

I eye him warily as he soaks some water into the shirt, turning to me and asking permission with his gaze. When I don't speak, he steps closer and squats in front of me, cringing as he dabs at the bloodied cuts on my skin, expecting me to flinch.

I've been hurt by experts, so a bit of brick rash isn't going to bother me.

"You don't need to do that," I grumble, but he snorts and glances up at me.

"Like fuck. I didn't mean to mark you like that. I didn't even think…"

"I said it's fucking fine!" I snap, confusion shining in his eyes as I step back, needing to get away from him.

The guilt weighing on my shoulders is making me angry, and I clench my fist, letting my nails bite into my palms to draw me out of it. It isn't working though, and more images of my guys flash through my mind.

They aren't my guys, for fuck's sake!

The guy touches my arm, and I pull it from his grip like it's a snake.

"Don't fucking touch me. Get the fuck out of my face," I warn, and surprisingly, he steps back.

"I just…"

"Fuck off. We're done here," I grind out through my teeth, turning to leave, but he darts around me, halting my escape. I go to yell at him, but I stop as he grabs a stack of bills from his pocket, offering them to me.

"Here."

I snatch them, ignoring how his eyes watch me with worry. I don't want his pity or whatever the fuck he's feeling. "Thanks."

"My name's…"

"I don't give a fuck, get out of my way before I gut you like a fucking fish," I snarl, and thankfully, he moves aside and lets me leave, guilt nipping at my heels the entire way home. Out of all the men who've ever left their scent on my body, his was the one I wanted to scrub off the quickest in the shower.

I'm fucked up, it's official.

My body aches like a motherfucker. Santos really got me good last time. If being on the receiving end of his fists is the way to keep him contained, I'll fucking do it daily, and I pretty much have been. If he loses it now? We'll all be screwed. I don't want to be cleaning up after him if he goes off and massacres a bunch of people, looking for an escape from his pain.

I can't fault him though; I'm not handling Selene being gone well either. The one reason I'm happy to be Santos' punching bag is because I deserve it. How did we let her sneak off and run like that? Losing her is killing us all slowly, and even though Zander seems alright, it will be slowly eating away at him that she's left us behind.

I am getting worried about Blaze, we can't risk him losing himself on the road, but he'd been right to go alone. We'd only slow him down when he's hunting, but I hate that he has to do it on his own. I can't worry too much about him though, I have to leave that for Zander. I have enough on my plate while I watch Santos lose his shit. He's currently beating his fists into the boxing bag without gloves on, his knuckles already split and bleeding all over the material, but the stubborn fucker won't stop. I tried to stop him ten minutes ago, but he nearly knocked me out with a crack to my jaw, then went back to wailing on the bag as if I'd never interrupted him.

I get comfortable in a chair in the corner, tossing him a towel to clean his fists with once he's dead on his feet, panting as he drops onto the floor in front of me. He wipes the fabric over his face to mop up the sweat, then he presses it against his busted knuckles, the blood soaking into the light blue material.

"You know not to get in my way, fuckface," he growls, but there's no heat in his words. He's worn himself out, so for that I'm grateful.

"I know. I'm sorry I give a shit about you, asshole," I snort, his eyes lifting to mine and showing me the emotions consuming him. He's hurting, more than I've ever seen, but for once it isn't a pain I can take away by killing or torturing some bastard.

I never thought a woman could worm her way into his heart, let alone all our hearts, and her silence is deafening. If she fucking called every day to say she was alright and missed us, maybe Santos wouldn't be so devastated. Maybe, my heart wouldn't be breaking as I watch my best friend create a void between us that's slowly becoming an ocean wide.

"I want to go and get her, man. We have to," he says softly, but he knows it's no use. We have to play this smart, not with force. I sigh and stand from my chair, dropping to the floor beside him and sitting cross-legged.

"We're all hurting without her, but she'll hate us if we drag her back home, demanding she do as she's told," I explain for the hundredth fucking time, but his lip lifts in a snarl, his eyes flashing with anger.

"I don't care if she hates me, as long as she hates me here."

"You do care if she hates you, so shut the fuck up. If she looks at you with disgust or hate, it will eat you alive. I promise we'll get her to come home, but we need to make sure she's dealt with her demons first. We have to let her go so she'll come back," I say through my teeth, hating the taste the words leave in my mouth. "I don't care if you have to lay into me every fucking day to release your emotions."

"D, you can't be my punching bag forever. You don't deserve any of my anger," he grunts, but I clap his sweaty shoulder with my hand, making him hold my gaze.

"Watch me. I fucking love you, you stupid prick. I'm here in any way you need me to get through this, and I'll be right here when our girl comes home to help you remind her where she belongs."

"Tag team?"

"I'll even let you take charge of me too," I promise, a sudden calmness swirling in his eyes as he finally gives me a soft smile.

"Is that your way of asking me to fuck you? Just gotta ask, bro. I'll plow your ass like a field," he teases, a chuckle leaving me.

"You wish, fuckface. Go shower, I want to go get burgers and turn in early for the night. We can call Blaze bright and early and make his day. I bet that fucker is missing us, don't you think?"

"No doubt," he grins, getting to his feet and helping me stand. "Thanks, bro."

"You know I've got you," I reply lightly, knowing he needs to hear that I'm not going anywhere. Selene is getting spanked hard for abandoning us. My hand is already itching to feel the crack against her skin.

Chapter Seven

Blaze

Did she really disappear down a fucking alley with a guy? I know he's not a target because I've been watching her and he's the one that approached her this time. What the fuck is she doing? I know what she's supposed to be doing and this is not it. She's been gathering information on the missing children and prostitutes and in doing so, has had to walk these streets late at night. But never has she disappeared down a fucking alley. I swear I'm going to kill the bitch.

I get out of the car and jog across the street, ignoring the hoots from a few girls at the corner. I stand at the mouth of the alley and hear voices bleeding out, making my jaw tighten. What the fuck are they talking about and why the fuck did they need to go down an alley to do it?

I step inside and press myself to the brick wall, my nose is immediately assaulted with the smell of sex. I can hear them, and I am stunned into place, my mouth drying. I know her lifestyle and I know the things she does to get the information she needs, but this is different. He wasn't a target and right now he's a client, in the middle of a filthy alley. Like she couldn't wait to take him to a car or his place, it had to be done here with the fucking rat shit.

I want to rip his dick off and force it down her throat, that's how fucking angry I am. My whole body is shaking, and my teeth are clattering together as if it's the middle of winter, only it's stiflingly hot here in Nevada. My vision blurs around the edges and I can feel the thumps of my rapid heartbeat, pulsing around my skull.

I step up beside a dumpster and listen to every moan, even when she cries out with her release. I crouch down and try to breathe as she comes again, my hand curving around the knife at my waist. Yeah, she clearly wants to die. She just handed over a piece of herself that belongs to the guys and me.

I hear them talking and I hear the rustle of clothing. The noises registering but my thoughts overpowering all the rest. I can feel myself slipping and I know of only one way to bring myself back. She better pray I get my head together or else I will be shipping her heart back home to Santos, he'll want a fucking piece of it after this. I hear her voice growing louder and my brows crash together at the sound. Is he forcing her to do something?

Then, they appear in front of me, briskly walking out of the alley, and hooking an immediate right. I hate what's happening, but I can't stop the smile that curves over my face. I'm going to finally hunt.

I give them a minute to pull ahead and then I fly out of the alley, following the bob of my girl's blonde head. They stop and I watch as he pulls his shirt off, wetting it with the spout that's connected to the brick building. What the fuck is he washing? Again, the pulses start, and I can't control the step I take forward. It's getting harder and harder to keep myself together. The sound of her snapping at him is the only thing that stops me from carving them into pieces, right here on the fucking street.

I watch as she rushes off and the pretty boy stands there, looking like he just lost his puppy. Well, he's about to meet a full-grown dog. I stalk forward, grabbing him by the hair, and taking him down the next alley. He tries to fight me but the only way he's getting away is if his scalp detaches from his fucking skull.

"What are you doing?" he snaps, "who are you?"

I throw his puny body into the wall and bend down to look into his eyes, "you were just fucking my girl."

"The prostitute?" he looks incredulous, and I smack him hard across the face.

"Her name is Selene, and she wasn't yours to touch."

"Look man," he holds up his hands, his skin growing paler by the minute, "she didn't tell me she was taken."

"I know," I smile, feeling giddy inside, "she'll be punished for that, too."

I grab his small neck in my large hand and squeeze, watching as his eyes begin to bulge. He claws at my wrist with his stubby fingers but it's not going to do a damn thing. I let go of him and when he bends over to suck in a choking breath, his throat meets my knife. The tip slips right in and when he tries to come back up, I hold his head down with my other hand. I force him down until my knife's serrated tip pokes out of the back of his neck and I can hear the gurgles of his blood, choking him.

I pull out my blade and watch as he falls to the ground, his small body shaking on the asphalt. I crouch down beside him and swipe my finger through the blood on my knife. I begin to draw on his chest as his eyes lose life and stand up to look down at my handy work. It looks close enough. I drew her scythe and then the word *reaped* beneath it. She might as well have killed him herself; it was all her fucking fault anyway.

I wipe the rest of the blood off onto the dead guy's wet shirt and stride out of the alley way. No one pays me any mind and if they saw me go in there with someone and now leave on my own, they don't say anything about it. Maybe that's how it is around here, people see these things all the time, and it's normal. I don't care either way.

I head back to my car and start it up, heading back towards Selene's. I need to make sure her ass is home and not out sucking another asshole's dick tonight. I check out my hands as I drive and exhale in relief, I'm no longer on the cusp. That kill ensures that Selene will live another night.

I pull up to her decrepit apartment building and shake my head at the sight, she is attracted to danger. I climb out and head around to the side of the building, jumping up to grab the fire escape ladder. I haul it down and quickly climb up, peering into other apartments on my way. There's a few crackheads and a couple of families in this building, an eccentric group. I get to the sixth floor and stand in front of her window, the yellowing lace blowing in the breeze. She leaves her window open most of the night and the only thing separating her from anyone is a screen.

I know she can take care of herself, but I can't help but think she's begging for trouble, anything to give her the high I know she gets from a fight or a kill. Just like me. I hear her shower running and I pull out the screen, like I've done so many other times. I step inside her living room and head straight for the bathroom, I want to drag her out by her wet head. As I reach for the door, the sound of a dying animal hits my ears, did she bring a cat in there? Just as I'm convinced that she's killing cats, I decipher words through the awful noise and chuckle when I realize she's singing. Damn, that's awful.

I step back and go into her bedroom; the light begins to flicker. It's a cheap ass place and I snarl when I see a blow-up mattress on the floor. I'm pissed at her, but I don't want her living in these conditions. I find her suitcase on the floor and lift the top with my boot, her awful singing still filling the space around me. I bend down and unzip a compartment, finding all her panties. I scoop them all out and toss them on the bed, pulling my knife from my waist.

I may not be killing her tonight, but I will leave her a message and hopefully she gets the meaning of it. I pick up each one bringing it to my nose. I do miss her.

Selene

Singing in the shower has always been a stress reliever for me and I know I have the voice of an angel. I take an extra-long shower this time, scraping the guy from my skin, and leaving long welts in places. The water runs cold long before I'm finished and I don't care, I will freeze to death before stepping out and taking the chance of still having his scent on me.

As soon as I wrap my body in a towel, I get the feeling I'm not alone, and I can swear I hear movement from the other room. I open the bathroom door slowly and look out into the apartment. It's a small place and I can see nearly every angle from where I'm standing. Nothing is in the apartment, but my bedroom door is closed, and I never close it, not even when I'm sleeping. I creep out and take quiet steps towards the room, cursing under my breath when I realize my knife belt is in there. I was in such a rush to scrub him off me that I didn't take it into the bathroom. I always have it with me. I slowly turn the handle and shove the door open quickly, hoping to startle anyone that may be inside. The door bangs off the drywall and sinks inside, creating a hole I know my deposit will cover.

The room is empty but what I find sends a chill down my spine. Someone was definitely here. I step towards my bed, picking up a pair of panties, and gasping when I see what's been done. There's a large cut through the crotch and when I look to my bed, every one of my panties are scattered there. I lift each one and see they all have the same cut, my heart pounding furiously. This stalking shit has gone on long enough and now I need it to end. I quickly change into a track suit, without underwear, and step back out into the main room.

I check the door and it's still locked tight from the inside, that leaves the fire escape. I stride over to the window and find it open wide, the curtains sucked outside. The screen is sitting neatly outside leaning against the brick like it was left for me to find. Almost as if they are warning me of the potential danger of using this window. They could've come into the bathroom and gutted me while I showered, but they didn't. I was ripe for the taking and still they chose to leave me a warning instead.

This was either an extremely sick person or someone I know, and honestly that means they could very well be both. If they thought they could scare me, they're so completely wrong and don't know me at all. I get dressed and throw on my trench, strapping my belt around my waist. I thought my night was over, but I guess it's not, I should thank the fucker for pulling me out of my funk.

I pop the screen back inside the window track and close the window, locking it tight. It'll never be opened again unless I'm sitting in front of it and watching for someone to try me. I know most people would move at this point, scared and feeling like their space was invaded. I'm a little happy that one: I can now go panty shopping, and two: my stalker has upped the ante. It was about time they grew into their balls.

I walk back to the front door and stop in the middle of the room, holding my nose in the air. A scent so familiar hits my nose and I breathe deeply, I know it. I just don't know where it's from. I commit it to memory this time and promise myself I won't forget it. The next time I smell it, my knife will be cutting into their flesh.

"You're back," the waitress says as I walk into the bar I was in earlier this week.

"I am," I grin at her and sit on a stool. "Whiskey please, on the rocks."

"You got it." She begins to fill up a tumbler with ice, "how was your night?"

I know she's wondering about if I've come across trouble in my night job.

"Pretty uneventful." I nod at the glass she hands me and take a large gulp.

The burn skates its way down my throat and warms my belly, I needed this.

"I have to warn you to be extra careful," she leans over the counter, staring into my eyes. "A regular hasn't shown up tonight and she's here every night."

"Does it happen to many of the girls that frequent here?" I raise a brow and sip my drink.

"Yes." She swallows thickly and looks around.

"Why do you think that is?" Another sip and I begin to look around at the faces.

"I don't know," she shrugs, "we are a popular spot."

"Looks like it." I nod.

"I just feel terrible because our boss is just beside himself with the connection." She tuts and begins to wash some glasses.

"Yeah, I can see how that would affect business," I tap my glass for a refill.

She fills my glass nearly to the brim and gives me a wink, "on the house tonight, unless you're a fish."

I laugh and gulp down almost half the glass, watching as her eyes widen, "I'll pay, trust me."

We both chuckle and the door chimes as someone walks in. I turn to see a young woman, her hair a thick mass of tight purple curls and her skin a beautiful ebony. My breath gets lodged in my throat when she throws the waitress a smile, she's so damn gorgeous.

"That's Aniyah."

"What's your name?" I tear my eyes off the girl and look at the waitress.

"Colleen." She smiles, her blue eyes twinkling. "Yours?"

"Selene."

"Is Aniyah in the same profession as I am?" I laugh when Colleen rolls her eyes.

"Yes, she is very sought after."

"I can see why," I toss another look at her over my shoulder.

"She's sweet but I wish she would stay away from here. It's not safe." She murmurs, looking worried as she dries the tumblers.

"Have you told her to be careful?"

"Yeah, but she's the boss' favorite." She huffs.

"His favorite?" I quirk a brow.

"Yeah, you know, for hire?" she rolls her eyes.

"Oh, he frequents the ladies of the night as well." I snort and she chuckles.

"He'd like you too," she nods, "he likes the tougher ones and you're certainly tough."

I can't help but wonder if the boss of this place is somehow a player in the women going missing. It would be a good front, having a bar that supports the women, and supposedly keeps them safe. Actually, it would be a brilliant idea.

"What's your boss' name?" I ask with a grin, "in case I want to offer my services."

She lets out a cackling laugh and I join in, taking another long gulp of my drink.

She stops laughing and wipes the corners of her eyes, "John Dempster."

"Pardon?" I lean over the bar; I couldn't have heard that right.

"John Dempster."

Chapter Eight

Zander

"She fucking what?" Santos barks, his fists tightening on his lap until his knuckles crack. Darius managed to calm him down once today, but by the look of this conversation, he'll have to do it again before the day is over.

"I said, she was working a client who wasn't a target. He was young, and the bastard was nice as fuck to her," Blaze growls through the phone, my eyes darting to Darius who snorts.

"Oh, that rat bastard was nice to her? She must have been terrified," he deadpans, and Santos scowls at his sarcasm. Selene is in deep shit when she gets home because Santos has completely passed the in-love phase and has nose-dived straight into possessive beast mode.

"He was all over her. I nearly stormed over to them and slit his throat when he made her come," Blaze continues, causing me to frown.

"Are you sure it was a client? She's not dating him, is she?" I ask, Santos instantly standing and almost knocking the table over as his leg swipes it.

"I'm going to fucking kill that piece of shit!"

"They exchanged money. She took off real fast though, so I have no idea what was going on. I bled that fucker dry in the street, so he won't be touching her again," Blaze snarls, relaxing Santos instantly, but worry seeps into my bones as Blaze rants about the entire thing.

He's losing it, just like I was worried about when the big prick left to go hunt her alone. He's not the type to go off on a rampage like that, so knowing he's left a body in the street is concerning.

"Do you need us to come to you, brother? You sound like you need it," I say carefully, knowing he can go off like a bomb when pushed. He chuckles, his voice appearing steady, but I can imagine his hands fisting in his lap as he fights for control.

"I'm fine. I can fucking handle the bitch perfectly fine on my own. If she gets too out of control, I'll cut her to pieces," he says through his teeth, a sigh leaving me as I rub my temples with my fingers. I swear I've had a constant headache since she left.

"That's what I'm worried about," I mutter, but he's not listening. He's too busy giving Santos all the fucking gory details about the nice dude he left bleeding. I should be relieved he killed the cunt before he could sway our girl into seeing him again, but I'm not. I'm too worried about what it means for Blaze.

When he finally hangs up, Santos pins me with his eyes, not hiding the crazy inside them.

"I think it's a good time to go after her. She's fucking people for the sake of it now, Zan. What if she's setting up a life for herself there? That's not the first person she's fucked and hasn't killed, she…"

"I'm aware, but the answer's still no. You heard Blaze, give him more time and he'll call us if he needs help," I answer, keeping my voice stern. I don't feel like being punched in the face repeatedly today, so I hope my tone is right.

As if sensing my wariness, Darius takes Santos' hand and tugs him back down onto the couch beside him, not letting his hand go.

"Remember what I said? She's coming home, so breathe. Blaze has her, and he's killing all those pieces of shit who fuck with what's ours, alright?"

I hope he doesn't kill anyone else, not because I give a fuck about those people, but because Blaze will slowly become the monster he hides below the surface, and nothing will bring him back from that.

Santos surprisingly lets out a steady breath and nods, squeezing Darius' hand in response, not using his words. We sit in silence for a while, until Santos excuses himself and heads to his room, quietly shutting the door behind him.

I look up at Darius and sigh. "He seems better."

"Only today. Tomorrow he'll probably be losing his shit again. I don't know how much longer I can hold the fucker back, Zan," he warns, genuine concern filling his eyes.

"Won't be long now, and we'll have our girl home," I promise, his throat bobbing as he swallows hard.

"I miss her."

"I miss her too, man."

I nearly spit my coffee as I watch the news over breakfast at the diner.

A body was found early this morning in an alley, my fucking reaper mark left on them in blood. I know I'm a little crazy, but I'm fairly sure I'd remember murdering someone before bed. I think. Am I losing it enough to forget killing some piece of shit?

Confusion pools in my stomach, my coffee tasting sour as I catch a glimpse of the body. It's covered by a blanket as the cops try to do their job. But that leg? Quite sure it's what had helped pin me to the wall and fucked the hell out of me last night. I left him there, staring after me. I know I didn't kill him.

"More coffee?"

I jolt as I realize the waitress is standing beside me, and I quickly plaster on a bright smile.

"Yes, please. Sorry, I zoned out for a second there. If that doesn't state I need a refill, nothing does," I joke, her lips quirking into a grin.

"I'm not a morning person myself, I get it. I'll be right back with your breakfast."

I thank her as she walks away, but my eyes catch on an image of a young woman on the TV. Left widowed after her husband - the nice guy - was murdered.

I knew that cunt was a fucking fraud.

The waitress returns with my breakfast, and I moan as I shovel a piece of bacon in my mouth, sucking my greasy fingers in after it. The waitress gives me an amused glance, but she leaves me to it, pretending she can't hear my orgasms while I eat.

Another lady looks at me with disgust, but I simply lick my fingers clean and give her a wink. "The food's fucking good, am I right? Remember to tip your waitress."

She scowls, turning away from me and letting me enjoy my breakfast without her judgement, not that I give a fuck. Would Darius have eaten bacon out of my coochie?

I pause at the mental image, my panties dampening as I close my eyes and a low groan leaves me.

Wait, stop that.

My eyes fly open and land on the woman who was scowling a second ago, and I make sure to stuff more bacon in my mouth like a savage, getting grease all over myself. Anything to stop the images of Darius burning into me any longer.

I focus on my eggs next, using my toast to mop up some yolk as it drizzles onto my plate.

"Good morning, Candy."

I startle for the second fucking time this morning, finding John standing beside my table. I quickly wipe my mouth with a napkin, giving him a bright smile.

"Mr. Dempster! It's lovely to see you! Please, join me!" I exclaim gleefully, when in reality I want to carve the fucker's eyes out of his skull and play beer pong with them.

He slides into the seat opposite mine, giving me an apologetic smile.

"I'm sorry I've been busy. I was hoping we could catch up again soon," he states, watching me as I practically lick my plate clean.

"I know you're a terribly busy man, sir. Whenever you can fit me into your schedule, I can be there," I beam, finishing my coffee so I can give him my full attention. He seems pleased with my statement, and he leans across the table to take my hand. He's lucky I wiped them on the napkin, or he'd get a handful of grease.

"I really enjoyed the other night. I'd love to do it again sometime," he murmurs, and I have to fight a scowl. I have to act like it has been a dream, so I flutter my lashes instead.

"I'd love to come over again. I really enjoy your company."

He gives me a look of approval, his eyes shining with desire.

"I'll be sure to get hold of you again this week then. Be careful when you're working, please. There've been a lot of people going missing late at night, and I'd hate for something to happen to you," he bullshits me, making me fake horror as I press my hand to my chest.

"I know, it's dreadful. Those poor people."

He turns the subject around to talk about himself, but I prefer that. He goes on about all his accomplishments, his new painting, and how successful the youth center and park are.

By the time we part ways, he promises to call within a day or two, and then he's gone. I know I need more information on John Dempster and his bar, but also about his preference for us ladies of the night.

I stand outside the bar and look up at the sign, "Good Times" it reads, and I try not to snort. *I bet it is, John.* I head inside and see

Colleen behind the bar, sidling up in what's becoming my regular stool. Her dirty blonde hair is up in a messy bun on her head and her large chest is threatening to spill out of her top.

"Selene," she nods, and I thank God, I gave her my real name. That way if her and John ever happen to speak about me, he won't connect that I'm the same person he's been seeing.

"Colleen," I grin, "the usual, please."

She hands me my whiskey on the rocks and lets out a huff, "there's so much death around here lately."

"I saw a few things on the news." I nod. "Looks like cops will be swarming the place soon."

"Yeah," she puffs out her breath, "a few of the girls are worried about that."

"I would be more worried about getting snatched or killed." I shrug. "Cops are easy enough to deal with, you're not dead."

"True."

"Has Aniyah been by tonight?" I ask, trying to sound nonchalant.

"Yes," she gives me a small smile, "she's fine."

"Do you expect her to be back tonight?"

"Yes," she grins, "are you in need of her services?"

"Something like that."

"Stick around for a few hours and you'll catch her." She heads off down the bar to pour a drink for another patron.

It's exactly two hours later when Aniyah shows up, her bright purple curls prominent in the darkened room. Tonight, she has on a silver tube top and a short leather skirt, her long legs gleaming. She really is so beautiful.

I get up off my stool and walk towards her, her brown eyes landing on me, and a small smile curving on her perfect cupid bow lips.

"My name is-"

"Selene," she cuts me off, her smile growing wider, "like the Greek Goddess of the Moon."

Her voice is like a melody, and I can feel myself softening, growing aroused with her words. "Yeah," my voice is husky and soft. I can see what makes John so infatuated with her, I want her, too.

"You're new around here," she steps in closer and fingers the lapel on my trench coat, "I know I would remember that face."

Her scent washes over me and I can't help the moan that escapes my mouth, I've never had such a strong reaction to a woman before.

"I did want to speak to you about a client," I shake my head to clear the fog, "could we sit down somewhere private?"

"You're taking time out of my night," her hand lands on her hip, "it'll cost you."

"Sounds good." I nod.

I follow her to a booth in the far corner of the bar and slide in across from her. She fiddles with the napkin holder and watches me from under her lashes.

"I heard you are close with the owner of the bar," I begin, straight to the point.

"John?" her nose crinkles on his name, "he's just a client who asks to spend time with me, we don't fuck."

"Oh," my brows crash together in confusion, "what do you guys do?"

"We talk," she shrugs, "sometimes he orders take out and we binge Netflix."

This is fucking strange.

"So, he has never tried anything?" I ask her.

"Nope," she shakes her head, "he's gay."

No, the fuck he's not. I rest my chin on my hand and try to figure out why he would tell her he's gay when he's clearly not.

"All the girls know he's gay," she chuckles, "he just hangs out with us some nights and pays us like a regular client. It gives us a break."

"All the girls that come by here?"

"Yeah," she leans forward, "I really think he's trying to protect us from whoever it is that's making the girls disappear."

Then it hits me like a ton of bricks, a gay man would make a girl feel completely comfortable, and her trust would be gained so easily. It must be John who's snatching them up.

REAPED

Chapter Nine

Blaze

Good Times.

I glare at the sign illuminated above the brick structure that Selene just entered. Good Times my fucking ass, this place is sucking up what little patience I have, and if she doesn't hurry up and get her shit together, it'll be her fault when the bodies begin to drop. I can't keep this up for too much longer and if she doesn't take my threat in her apartment seriously, I may have to slit her flesh next.

The place looks popular with many patrons flocking in and out, but I can't help but notice the number of prostitutes that frequent. I know they're prostitutes because I have been watching this strip and I never forget a face. I don't understand why they all congregate at this bar, and I know there must be a connection for Selene to be here, but what is it?

I pull up my hoodie and yank it down low over my face. It's a risk I'll be seen but I need to know the connection so I can speed this bitch along. We've been here too long, and the boys back home are losing their shit. If I fail at bringing her home, I'll probably have to kill them to retain my piece of mind.

I jog across the street and open the door to the bar, stepping into the bustling space. The music is booming from a jukebox and the lighting is dull, the darkness working in my favor. I sit at a booth in the front of the bar, sliding all the way into the wall, and I wait. I don't know where Selene is but I'm sure she'll appear and, in the meantime, I'll listen to the people around me.

"What can I getcha, sir?"

I look up and see a waitress standing with a hand on her hip, her face trying to see under my hood. Her face is plain, too thin lips, and a hooked nose. Not interesting at all.

"Soda water." I reply and avert my face. I hate nosy bitches.

"You came to the bar for soda water?" she chuckles.

"I came to the bar to get out of the house." I snap.

"Gotcha." She taps her fingers on the table. "I'll get your drink then."

She comes back and slides the glass across the table, the collected sweat on the outside wetting my hand. "On the house, sir." She huffs, "you let me know when you want a real drink."

I ignore her and she walks away with a tut, her attitude grating on my last frayed nerve. If I decide to start a fucking slaughter, she's first, then Selene. I rest back against the back of the booth and open my ears, letting the sounds assault my ear drums. As much as Tom Banks was abusive, he was also useful, and he taught me how to zero in on noises, drowning out others. I hear John's name and zero in on that conversation.

It's a woman with a beautiful voice and I wonder if she sings.

"John?" she pauses, "he's just a client who asks to spend time with me, we don't fuck."

Then I hear the next voice, knowing it's my girl, and my hand tightens around the glass. Of course, she's digging for information, and it bothers me how blatant she is about it. I listen in on their conversation and when I hear that John is gay, I let out a snort. No, he fucking isn't, I've seen the way he looks at my woman, and there's nothing gay about it.

I wonder if Selene is piecing everything together as well as I am, knowing that John owns this bar, and that he's capturing prostitutes on the promise that he would rather suck dick than eat a pussy.

She better hope she is because I can't keep up this guise for long, I want to kill John and Mack, then drag her ass home and watch the guys punish her. Santos will be the most interesting. I take a drink and swallow it down knowing that's not how this situation will go down. Selene wants to find her sister and I have a feeling Mack would know where she is, probably having transported her himself.

I finish my drink, and keeping my hood low, I stand to leave the bar. I've heard all I need and now I have to update the guys. I know our girl is tough, but I don't want her taking on John alone, he's a big fucking fish. I don't think I could take him on alone either.

"Leaving so soon?" The waitress purrs from behind the bar as I walk by. She does nothing for me and so I ignore her, throwing open the door with more force than necessary.

I need to figure out a plan before calling the guys. This needs to be handled perfectly.

The entrance to the bar bangs open and I snap my head around to catch the back end of a tall, well-built man leaving the joint. His stature looks familiar and my pussy clenches at the sight. Once the door shuts, I shake my head, and pull myself back into my conversation with Aniyah.

"I really wouldn't mind striking up the same deal with this guy." I lean in, "it's getting dangerous around here and spending time with a safe man like that sounds great."

"It is," she smiles. "I can introduce you."

"Can you?" I make sure the excitement is clear on my face.

"He's busy this whole week but he's asked me to meet him here next Tuesday."

That's eight days. I know I'm due to hear from him in a few days, but he only promised a phone call. Eight days gives me a good amount of time to come up with a plan, and I can't think of any other way than to surprise him with a visit one night, outing myself and him at the same time.

"That would be amazing, really." She has no idea just how much.

I throw down five hundred on the table - double what she asked for - and stand. Her eyes widen and she gives me a once over, stuffing the bills into her bra.

"Let me know if you ever want to hang out again." She winks and I can feel the wetness rush between my legs.

"I'll know where to find you." I bite into my lip and force myself to walk away. If I stay there with her, I'll be on my knees in no time, and working her pussy with my tongue.

I stride to the bar, trying to push back my wanton thoughts of Aniyah, and sit on my stool. I've drank too little or not enough, either way I'm ordering another, and I'll use it to drown my thoughts of pussy.

Colleen pours me a glass without my having to ask and I smile in thanks.

"We just had a weird customer," she puts the bottle of whiskey back, "I've never seen him before, and he ordered a soda water."

"Ew," I screw up my face, "that shit's like drinking no cellphone service."

She cackles loudly and nods, "yeah, he wouldn't show his face, but he was big and ominous."

"That's the one I saw stomping out of here." I take a sip, "did he say anything?"

"Nothing of importance."

"We'll have to keep an eye out." I gulp down my drink and toss some money on the counter, "I need to sleep off this hangover." I say as I stand. "I'll see you tomorrow."

"Be careful on your way home." She looks nervously at the door.

I nod and pull my trench's collar up around my neck, I wish someone would try and nab me. It's the surest way to find out what's going on, where my sister is, and satisfy my need to kill.

REAPED

Chapter Ten

Selene

It's my third night in a row at the bar and I have yet to see the stranger again. Colleen says he hasn't been back either and no one else has gone missing. Aniyah has been here each night and every time I see her, my body becomes more responsive. I don't know what it is about the woman with the bright purple hair, but I fucking want her, and I can't stop thinking about it.

I'm sitting in my regular stool, my eye on the door, and in walks Aniyah with a handsome man on her arm. She's wearing a purple off the shoulder top and a dark blue pair of skinny jeans. He's tall - not as tall as Blaze - maybe about Zander's height of six feet-two inches and his body is lean, nothing like my guys. He's got a swimmer's body, trim, and he's dressed in a pinstripe suit, pinstripe. None of my guys would wear that. I groan internally and try once again to push them out of my mind.

I watch as Aniyah leads him to the booth we were in yesterday and his black hair gleams unnaturally under the table lighting. It's such a contrast to his alabaster skin and I wonder if it's dyed.

"Colleen," I call out and she comes to stand in front of me, "who is that with Aniyah?"

"Don't know him."

"Does that hair look natural to you?" I ask and she snickers.

"Girl, let the man live, maybe he has greys."

"Or maybe he's changing his appearance?" I shoot her a look.

"Oh." She breathes.

"You know Aniyah," I begin, "how would she feel if I joined them?"

"I've seen the way she's been looking at you," she grins, "I'd say it'll be welcomed and by them both."

"Could you send their table a tray of Wet Pussy shots?" I ask her with a grin, "might as well make it known what I expect."

She throws her head back and cackles, "I don't know how I ever got through the nights without you here, Selene." Then she heads off down the bar to make the shots.

Ten minutes later, I follow Colleen as she carries the tray to the table, setting it down between Aniyah and the stranger.

"Selene wanted to send you guys some shots." She murmurs and Aniyah looks up at me with a smile.

"They're Wet Pussy shots," I tell them. "Colleen sure is shy to say it but not as much to make it."

Colleen chuckles and walks away with a blush spreading up her neck and face.

"Join us my Moon Goddess." Aniyah purrs, sliding over in her seat to make space.

I sit beside her and give the guy across from us another closer look. He's clean shaven and he has the most striking pale blue eyes, making him look even paler.

"Ah yes, Selene." He smiles and his pale pink lips flatten, showing straight, white teeth, "Moon Goddess. Very nice name."

"Thank you." I nod. I stare into his eyes unable to look away, his lashes look so unnaturally long and black. "I didn't mean to interrupt your night," I look at Aniyah, "I just couldn't seem to stay away."

Her dark eyes brighten, and she leans into me, pulling a piece of my hair with her fingers. "I'm glad."

I know I'm not imagining her interest in me, and this pull we have is getting harder to ignore.

"Will you be joining us tonight, Selene?" Stranger cuts in. *Oh right, fuck, I forgot about the Addams Family.*

"I don't know," I smirk at him, "Can you afford that, Mr.?"

"Angelo Gomez." He replies and I almost spit out my Wet Pussy. His name is Gomez? Like the fucking Addams family. This must be fake, right?

"Okay Mr. Gomez-"

"Angelo is fine." He cuts me off and I exhale with relief, I don't think I'd be able to call him Gomez with a straight face. "Money is never an issue."

I beam at him, showing all my teeth, and Aniyah links her fingers through mine. She leans in and presses her mouth to my ear, "I have been waiting for this."

I turn my head and brush my mouth against hers, "you have no idea."

I see Gomez Addams across the table lean in to watch us closely and I groan when Aniyah's tongue flicks against my lower lip. I wind my hand around her neck and haul her in, devouring her mouth with mine. Katy Perry was completely accurate, she tastes just like cherry Chapstick, and I don't think I can stop. She moans into my mouth, her tongue meeting mine, thrust for thrust.

A throat clears and I almost growl at the fucker sitting across from us, how dare he interrupt?

"Is this a regular thing?" he asks as we pull apart.

"No," Aniyah answers, breathlessly, "but I've been wanting her."

"I can see that." He squirms in his seat, and I would bet my last Wet Pussy that he's adjusting his cock in his pants.

I take my shot just as Aniyah leans over the table, "my pussy's wet and I want to eat hers, when can we get out of here?" I choke on the liquid and Aniyah rubs my back while looking at Angelo.

"Yeah, okay," he swallows thickly, looking between us with excitement in his eyes.

Same, dude.

He has a motel room on the ground floor, and I can see my shitty ass building a few blocks over. I hope he actually has enough money for this because it's going to be pricey. I take off my trench coat and hang it over the red velvet chair, then carefully unsnap my belt. I carefully remove it and place it over my jacket, hiding the fact that it's a knife.

"Would you two like a drink?" Angelo asks and I watch Aniyah strut across the room.

She stands in front of me, her purple curls glistening, and her eyes alight with passion, "no." She snaps sounding impatient and slams her mouth to mine.

I match her ferocity and one hand grabs onto her hair while the other snakes up her shirt. Her skin is so soft and we both moan at the contact. My fingers brush along the underside of her bra and she breaks our kiss to toss her shirt over her head. I do the same and then we're right back at each other. Our teeth clash and our bodies collide, the heat from her skin warming mine.

I've made out with girls before, I've even fucked them for money, but it's never been like this. No real feelings and never the overwhelming need to taste them. Pussy has never been something I sought after; right now, I would kill to taste hers. I unclasp her bra and break our kiss to pull it off her body. Her breasts bounce with the motion, and I can feel the fluid between my legs. I bend forward and take a brown nipple into my mouth, whimpering at the taste of her skin.

"Get on the bed," I hear her bark at Angelo as I make my way down her taut stomach and begin to unlatch her jeans.

She helps me pull them down, taking her panties with them, and as soon as I smell her arousal, my eyes sink back into my head. This can't be natural; she smells too fucking good. I drop to my knees and grab her thigh, hauling her leg over my shoulder. Her pussy spreads open and I spread it more with my fingers. She's fucking dripping wet, and I waste no time sucking it all into my mouth, reveling in her scream.

"Yes," she begins to grind against my face, "fuck my pussy with your tongue." I hear Angelo on the bed removing his clothes and then Aniyah has her hands gripping my hair, the force ripping out a few strands.

I sink my tongue deep inside her and use my nose to rub against her clit. Her hands pull on my hair to bring me closer and I replace my tongue with two fingers, sucking her clit between my teeth.

"Oh fuck, Moon girl," she moans, "that's it."

I can feel her juices along my chin and cheeks, but I don't stop. I want to swallow every drop from her. I pump my fingers faster and nip down on her clit, her pussy walls clenching around.

"I'm coming," she screams out, "fuck, Selene."

"Jesus," I hear Angelo from the bed, the slap of his cock loud in the room.

She comes with a gush of wetness that trickles over my cheeks and into my hair, some dripping to the floor.

"Holy shit," she moans as I continue to lap it up.

I finally release her, and she stumbles a bit, her eyes glazed over and satisfied. I stand and wipe my face into my shirt, looking over at Angelo. I startle when I see the stark white of his pubic hair, everything suddenly making sense. His pale skin and dyed hair, he's an albino. Fuck this is a first, it really is, I have never had an albino. His cock is large, and he has a Jacob's Ladder running down the underside, exciting me even more.

I can't wait to bounce on that.

I scramble out of my clothes as Aniyah crawls up his body, her long purple nails scraping his pale skin, and sucking his cock down her throat. She really is the fucking equivalent to a Hoover, and I have nothing on her skills. I'm fucking jealous because I want her mouth on me, not Angelo. She releases his cock with a pop and looks at me over her shoulder.

"Get over here."

I've never moved so fast in my life, and I watch as Aniyah rolls off the bed, my stomach instantly dropping with disappointment.

"Suck his cock." She demands and I eagerly do so, wanting to taste her on his skin. There's a lingering taste of cherries and I moan around him, causing him to jerk in my mouth. The bumps of his piercings knock against my teeth, and I admit, I can't wait to have them inside me.

Blaze's pierced tip was amazing so I can only imagine what this will feel like. My stomach begins to sour with the thought of Blaze, and guilt begins to bubble inside me until I feel my ass cheeks being spread. I continue to stroke Angelo's cock, my palm bumping over the piercings, and look over my shoulder at Aniyah. She gives me a quick wink and then her face disappears between my legs, her purple hair the only thing I see.

When her tongue sinks into my pussy, I gasp, and my hand pauses on Angelo's dick. He makes up for my lack of movement by pumping up into my palm and I lose myself in the feel of Aniyah nipping and sucking on my pussy lips. I hear a high pitch whine and shock myself when I realize it's coming from me. She sinks two fingers inside me, and I am almost embarrassed by the noises my pussy makes as she fucks me with them.

Once she has a good rhythm going, I lean back down, and take Angelo's cock into my mouth. Paying extra attention to that rough ridge under the head. He begins to pant and jerk in my mouth and I'm on the edge as Aniyah works my pussy. Then I feel her flattened tongue glide along my asshole, and I gasp around Angelo, choking when he pushes upward.

Aniyah chuckles behind me and continues lashing her tongue against my rear hole, then pushing it inside. The feel of her spreading me with her tongue and fucking me with her hands has me falling over the edge, my pussy clamping down on her hard. I black out and scream her name, stars exploding behind my eyes. When I come around, I have tears soaking my cheeks from the intensity and my body is trembling.

I'm fucking keeping her.

I won't lie, it was hot watching my girl eat out another and then vice versa. I heard her scream from my parked car in front of the motel room. The part that disturbed me was her sucking that asshole's dick and then watching as her pussy sank down over it, all those piercings making her eyes roll back in her head.

Now, the Albino fucker must die, only this time Selene will be getting a bolder message. She clearly isn't fucking getting the picture.

The two girls leave together, sharing an Uber, and I wait a few minutes while the guy stays on the bed, unable to move or even wash his dick. Fucking gross. When I see his chest moving in a slower rhythm, I know he's fallen asleep, and I also know the dumb fuck didn't get up to lock the door. It's like it's all meant to be, and this is what I'm supposed to be doing.

I let myself into his room and the snores are reverberating off the walls, the sounds akin to a chainsaw. The smell of sex is so fucking thick in here and it makes my cock harden, despite the circumstances. I miss her and it's supposed to be my dick she's riding.

I walk up to the top of the bed and look down into his face. I hate that he's sleeping here, sated by my girl's pussy, and enjoying the aftermath like he owns it. Too bad he'll never get it again, or any other pussy for that matter.

When his mouth opens again on another Earth-shaking snore, I slam one of my hunting knives down inside of it, stopping only when it sinks into the mattress under his head. His eyes snap open and he begins to tremble, he's now a quadriplegic. I stroll down to the middle of the bed and stop adjacent to his flaccid cock and stare at it as it lays against his thigh. Selene really seemed to love those piercings, maybe I will get that for her. I'm the only one out of us four that could take that pain anyways.

His body continues to jerk, and I grab his limp dick, studying the piercings closer. I can get this for her. I pull out my phone and snap a picture, I'll need to show the piercer exactly what I want. Then I grab the other knife strapped to my waist and slip it through the base of his cock. It easily cuts through the flesh, leaving behind a clean bleeding stump. I walk back up and see his eyes are closing, he's on the brink of death. I pull my other knife out of his throat and wipe it on the bed, then replace it back into the holder. He'll be dead within a few minutes. At least he was fucked well before he died.

I use the bloody end of his cock in my hand and draw her scythe. Santos is going to love this.

I pull up to her apartment building and see she has the lights on. Maybe she brought her new friend home. I yank on the fire escape and listen as it drops with a clatter, uncaring if she hears it above. Maybe it's time she finds out I'm here.

I climb up quickly, the metal shaking beneath me, and the sound rattling inside my head. I reach her apartment and look inside the window, not bothering to hide, and not worried about her killing me. I don't see her anywhere, but I do see an opened bottle of wine and a few glasses. They probably moved to the bedroom. I pull on the window and chuckle when I find it locked. I pull out my knife and run it between the trim and the glass, popping the old-style lock without issue.

I yank up the pane of glass and step inside, hearing giggling coming from her bedroom. I pull out the Ziplock bag with the severed cock and open it, emptying the contents on her small kitchen counter. She won't miss it. Then I take a seat on her sofa, so sick of sitting in my car, and rest my head on the back of it. This place smells like her and it toys with my senses. My cock hardens and I undo my pants just as I hear breathless moans coming from the bedroom.

I grab my swelling cock in my hand and give it a hard squeeze, a drop of cum dripping from the tip. I smear it around the head and begin a punishing rhythm. I hate masturbating but the bitch has driven me to it. I feel my balls tighten just as Selene screams out to her god, or the bitch between her legs, and I cum all over her small table in front of her couch.

I shake off any lingering drops onto the floor and tuck myself away. I head back for the window, deciding to close it this time, and ensure she doesn't screw it shut. I skip back down the steep metal stairs, my mind once again clear, and my need to release sated.

It was a productive night.

Chapter Eleven

Santos

I can't wait to drag my fucking blade across Selene's perfect skin, carving my mark into her flesh to warn others away. Every time Blaze updates us about her, my blood boils, and a primal need to claim her in front of every other man breaks through to the surface, dragging me back to my angry pit of violence.

She's blurring the lines between work and pleasure, and I don't fucking like it one bit. Half the people she's been with lately are giving her pleasure, pleasure that they have no right to give her. She belongs to us, no one else.

Darius' fingers tighten on my knee, drawing me back to the conversation and away from my violent thoughts, and I can't help but appreciate how attentive he is to my emotions. He always knows exactly what to do or say to me.

"So, she's got a new friend?" Zander states calmly, and he's lucky I don't punch him in the face for how in control of his emotions he's been since she left. I don't like her having a new friend, that means having ties in different places, and the only tie she needs is to us.

Blaze scoffs, his voice blunt as usual. "If you wanna call a whore that, then sure. After what I saw and heard last night, I'd say they're a little closer than that."

I sit up straighter, glaring at the phone that's sitting on the coffee table in front of us.

"Wait, you think they're becoming involved or something? She can't fucking love that bitch, she…" I am going to fucking kill some cunt. I don't give a fuck if it has a set of tits, I'll still kill it.

"I didn't say they're falling in love, dick head, I'm just stating that they're close. Wine glasses on the table and giggling from the bedroom is usually a good sign that the girls were off the clock and winding down after a hard day of dick," he grunts, confusion pulsing through me.

"Wait, you got that close to where she's staying, and you didn't snatch her up and throw her in the car? What the fuck, Blaze?!" I bark, literally hearing his eyes roll through the phone.

"Close? I sat on her couch and hung out for a while."

"She just let you hang out and didn't try to gut you?"

"I never said she knew I was there," he answers, and Zander cracks a smirk.

"She's going to kill you when she realizes you've been inside her house. You know that, right?" he asks, but Blaze laughs, not sounding amused.

"The cunt can try, but I'm close to killing her with my bare hands if she doesn't shut her fucking legs."

"Santos," Darius says quietly under his breath, warning me to calm down. My fists bend tightly into balls, and I'm this close to shoving my feet in my shoes and strapping some ammo to a vest. If she wants me to come and get her, I'll be coming in hot and fucking fast.

I relax my hands, ignoring how Zander's eyeing me like I'm a wounded dog. He knows if anyone gets too close right now, I'll fucking bite a chunk out of them, so he's not wrong to stay back.

I let out a breath, turning my attention to the phone. "Anything else to report? What's that John fucker doing? Is he still trying to fuck her? Can I help you blow his fucking brains across the pavement yet?" I growl, calming a fraction as Darius agrees.

"Yeah, need us to come gun anyone down yet?"

"Stay fucking put or I'll be the one gunning you fuckers down. She's not done with him apparently, or he'd already be dead as a Dodo. I left her a gift, so hopefully it encourages her to wrap up her bullshit and get her ass home," Blaze says casually, Zander groaning in response.

Blaze gives interesting gifts, that's for sure.

"What did you do?" Zander demands, making me chuckle, the weight on my chest lightening at knowing Blaze is on my side. That girl is ours, and it's about time she fucking knows it.

"I possibly helped some albino fuck dismantle his sex stick. Since Selene loved it so goddamn much, I left it for her as a memento," he replies smoothly, a smile of victory in his tone. I hoot with laughter at the image I get, despite the fact he said our girl enjoyed it.

"You freaky fucker! Did you leave her a floppy dildo?!"

"I did. I hope she shoves it up her ass and fucks herself silly, too," he grunts, seeming distracted. As much as I wish to be the one who causes bloody mayhem and drags her home, I'll be more than happy for Blaze to go ape-shit and fuck everyone up. That fucker is a beast when let loose.

"So, what do we do about this chick she's spending time with? Can we kill her?" I grin, and Darius chuckles from beside me.

"Down, boy."

"Please!" I beg, making Zander and Blaze both snort. They should just appreciate the fact that I'm asking and not diving straight into my own agenda. It's still in the cards.

"You're a dick," Blaze mutters, causing my grin to widen.

"How? You wanna lick me, big boy? Do I excite you like a big peen? It's a new kink, but I'll try to lay still while you run your tongue over me. Oh! Want me to bring some maple syrup? How about whipped cream in a can?" I offer, curses spilling from him before he hangs up, apparently sick of my bullshit.

Darius raises an eyebrow, his voice low. "You know, one of these days, that big bastard's going to take you up on your stupid offers, just to spite you," he warns, making me laugh.

"I've never come across something I haven't liked. Other than that time I tried to put my knife blade first into my butt. I don't recommend trying that at all," I scowl, remembering the tiny cut being a major problem all week. I was terrified of pooping for days.

Zander stands, giving me a level look. "Trust me, no one was hoping to try that, you fucking psycho."

"What are you going to do to Selene when we get her back, Zan?" I ask, not giving a fuck if he thinks I'm crazy. Crazy people don't know they're crazy, and I know I am, so therefore, I'm not crazy.

"It's probably easier to tell you what I'm not going to do to that bombshell when I get her under me again," he shrugs, but I see it in his eyes before he can hide it. He's hurting more than he's letting on, just like I know he is.

The gunshots sound like heaven as I raise my gun, firing at the targets down the range. We are all worked up and anxious, so I decided it was best to let out some of our moods before we ended up killing someone for real.

Santos dragged a pile of weapons along, and so far, he's probably used more bullets than our enemies fucking own. He's re-enacting some of our shoot outs, a small smile quirking my lips up as he loudly and dramatically screams *pew pew* through the range, dodging and weaving imaginary bullets in the process.

Darius seems more relaxed as he fires a few rounds, hitting his targets with ease, then glancing over to check on Santos regularly. We needed this more than I thought, and I'm so glad I forced them into coming. Not that Santos needs an excuse to shoot at shit, because that fucker was out the door and getting in the car before I even finished my sentence about the afternoon plans.

It feels weird without Blaze and Selene here, and I force myself to think about something else as the familiar pit settles in my stomach. Our family is fractured, and I'm hurting for all my brothers. We need to work a job or something to keep us busy, but I have no idea what to do.

There are a few people on my shit list, but I need a clearer head to handle those. Nothing major, just rapists and skin sellers, but I can't afford for us to make mistakes if we aren't using our heads right. Santos will gun down half the fucking neighborhood once he starts, and even though Darius is usually well put together with his emotions, he's slowly snapping too.

Between containing Santos' demons as well as his own broken heart, the cracks are starting to show, and I'm worried about what he'll do if given the chance.

I can't have them running loose around the streets, or we'll have a massacre, and I can't clean that up alone while they wage war on the town.

"Take that, you pissy pants motherfucker!" Santos screams, catching my attention as he literally dives forward to duck and roll, holding his gun out and firing three shots at his target that is practically one big fucking hole now.

"Why is he a pissy pants?" I snort, a sadistic smirk taking over his sweaty face.

"Well, he's a pissy pants now that I'm done with him. One glance my way, and his dick was whizzing right down his leg and warming his socks! Don't distract me!" He laughs manically, suddenly dropping to the ground and dramatically clutching his chest. "I've been hit! You fuckbag, you got me hit!"

Darius is laughing loudly, and I simply roll my eyes.

"I'll fucking shoot you myself in a second, drama queen. There's plenty of distractions out in the real world, so I'm just helping you prepare," I shrug.

"Lies!" He exclaims, aiming his gun my way playfully to fake shoot me, his eyes going wide as he accidentally taps on the trigger and sends a bullet whizzing right past my fucking head. "Oopsie Daisy!"

"Santos!" I snap, but he's on his feet and darting behind Darius, using him as a human shield.

"Sorry!" He grins, moving to fake shoot me again, but he jerks back as I shoot at their feet lazily.

"I'm this close to cutting off your fucking balls," I promise, holding my thumb and pointer finger apart the tiniest amount, and Darius can't help but join in with the fun.

"As long as he touches your balls, right, San?"

"Ooh, Daddy Zander wants my balls?" Santos says and fakes a groan, my stomach twisting at his words. If anyone gets to call me Daddy, it's my blonde psychotic sex kitten.

Just get your ass home, Selene.

Darius and Santos are wrestling, thankfully without guns in their hands, and I sigh as I lean back against the wall. I need Blaze home too, before I drown in childish bullshit from the other two. We have a balance, and this separation is fucking with it.

My muscles hurt in every way and it's so fucking delicious. I stretch out and hear a soft purr beside me, smiling when I realize my new obsession stayed the night.

"Are you smiling at me?" her voice is like liquid sex, "I can feel it." She presses her full tits into mine and drapes an arm over my waist.

"I am." I chuckle and bury my face into her curls, "do you want some coffee?"

"Sure, in like twenty minutes, let me sleep more." She husks out and I can feel myself growing wet at her tone.

I slip out of bed and throw on a robe, quietly stepping out of the room. I walk across the hall to the bathroom and relieve myself. I'm sore down there too and I moan when I think about why. Aniyah used a few toys on me, and I can honestly say she looks sexy as fuck with a strap on. I walk out to the kitchen and rub the sleep from my eyes, opening the fridge for the water to start the coffee. I have one of those old school percolators and the smell that fills the apartment when it's on is divine.

The scent of coffee permeates my fog addled brain and I moan into the open tin. *Fuck, that's so good.* I take out a few scoops and set up the machine, turning to look across the room. My eyes zoom in on an object sitting on my counter and the spots of blood around it, something glinting in the light along its length. I'm instantly awake and my stomach threatens to push its bile up my throat.

I take a single step and dry heave into the room, recognizing what's laying on the counter. There's no way; it can't be. Only, I know it is, I know those piercings, and even though the skin is now grey, I know it was once an unnatural white. My heart stutters in my chest when I look back to my bedroom, Aniyah can't see this. I grab a bag from under my sink with some disinfectant wipes. I slip the bag over my hand and grab the appendage, sealing it inside the plastic. I tie it and throw it into my garbage, gagging at the soft feel of the flesh. I wipe down the blood and spray air freshener into the room, cursing at the nerve someone has.

The bedroom door opens a few minutes later and I exhale with relief that she wanted to sleep in. How the hell would I explain that I have a psycho stalker? And that they're accelerating by killing the men I've slept with. My stomach drops when I look at Aniyah, will they kill her next?

"Oh my," she groans coming into the kitchen, "that smell is amazing."

I know she won't let me crowd her and if I even suggest her not going anywhere without me, she'll cuss me out. Last night when I told her I wanted to keep her, she laughed and said that this was just fun, and one day we'll go our separate ways. It broke my heart but she's right, this isn't a forever thing. So how do I tell her to watch her back and to stay away from me?

I nod at her statement and grab her a mug, filling it with the black elixir. I watch as she sips and moans at the taste, my pussy clenching with want. I push it down and ready myself to pull away, I need to make sure she stays alive. She strolls to my couch and sits down as I fill half my cup with creamer.

"What the fuck?" she murmurs, and I freeze, looking up at her. What else is there? "Did you have a client over last night?"

"I don't bring clients here," I tell her as I walk over to see what she's inspecting.

"That tells a different story," She smirks and points at the table.

I look down and my stomach flips once more, cum. There's cum all over my small coffee table and a lot of it. It's drying but still thick globs dotting the surface. I look at the window and see it's shut. The front door is also shut and locked.

"It looks fresh too, unless..." she sniffs at it, "nope, that's definitely cum." When she looks up at me, she must see the confusion and anger. "Someone was in here without your knowledge." She stands and looks around, "do you think whoever is taking the girls is following us?"

"I don't know," I whisper, my voice shaking with anger. "We should get you home." I don't want her here any longer. This person might just catch on to how important she is to me, and she could be the next one with my scythe on her body.

It's clear now that someone is killing the men I sleep with, and I can't stop the image of Santos sliding through my brain. It can't be them; they don't know where I am, and they can't track me. I don't have the same phone, I don't use credit cards, and I didn't leave the ledger behind. My Reaper symbol and the mutilated bodies tell another story though.

I shake my head and let those thoughts go. I just miss them and maybe a piece of me is hoping they found me. I think that's why I'm clinging to Aniyah and looking for some sort of attachment. Even though I went through most of my life without any, I miss the few attachments I had, and I can't seem to purge my mind of them.

Aniyah sits unperturbed by the drying bodily fluids in front of her and finishes off her coffee. I guess the sight of cum wouldn't make her squeamish since that's a huge part of our jobs. Still, seeing her undisturbed about someone being in here and following us is pissing me off. I want her to be fearful so she will watch herself better, I can't be there to protect her all the time.

She pulls out her phone and stares at the screen, "my ride's here." She stands, "will I see you at the bar later?"

"Yeah." I nod as she leans in to kiss me.

She grabs her purse and saunters out my door, her ass swinging seductively from side to side. How can I keep her safe when even her walk screams *come fuck me*? I throw myself back down onto the couch, staring at the cum, and fisting my hands. I don't know if I locked the window or door, and with the rush I was in last night to have Aniyah's pussy in my mouth, it's possible I didn't. I'm acting stupid and not myself here, my emotions running the show. I changed the moment I gave myself over to the guys and now I only have myself to blame as I look to fill the void that leaving them behind has caused.

I turn on the small tube TV I have in the corner, and I only have three free channels to surf through. One shopping channel, one kid's channel, and one local news. I turn to the local news and take a sip of coffee, spewing it across the cum table when I see the image on the screen. There's a one million dollar reward out for anyone that can locate the Reaper Killer. A close up of Angelo's pale white skin is on the screen with my scythe drawn into it with blood.

Someone is trying to get my attention.

REAPED

Chapter Twelve

Blaze

Selene has been subdued the last few days and I must admit, kind of boring. Not that I want her fucking random people, but I do miss her stabby ways. She's been walking up and down the strip, speaking to hookers, and watching the clients that come to pick them up. She hasn't hung out at the bar and only pops in and out, probably assuring her friends she's alive and well, for now.

I haven't been back inside her apartment because I know she's probably been more vigilant, but I did see her buy a new bolt lock and a window bar from the local hardware store. I can still work my way around a window bar if need be. All in all, things have been quiet and we're both waiting patiently for John to come back around. He's been busy clearing out the shipment I watched him receive the other night and last night was his last *export*. I feel bad that I couldn't help those people, but I had to stay the course; just as Zander likes to say, we can only do our best.

I'm waiting for the moment he contacts my girl because I know he will, and I think tonight is the night. I saw the way he watched her, and I can't imagine him putting it off longer than necessary. The sun begins to set and it's about the regular time Selene begins her patrol, only she's not coming out. I look up at her apartment and see that the lights are on, and everything looks quiet, but why hasn't she made her way down yet?

I'm about to get out and investigate when I see the BMW pull up to the curb. The windows are tinted but I know John's car well enough. I slide down in my seat and watch as a few moments later, Selene slinks out of the door. I'm shocked she had him pick her up here, it's fucking dangerous and reckless for him to know where she lives, what's she planning?

"Candy!" He exclaims as he gets out of the car and rounds the front to embrace her.

"Candy?" I mumble with disgust. The fuck kind of stripper name is that?

She's whispering something in his ear and smiling when he kisses her cheek enthusiastically. She's wearing a long black cocktail dress, strapless, and a slit that nears her fucking hip. I growl when I see it flap gently in the wind. He opens her door and before she slides inside, her eyes land on my car. It's the first time in a long time that my heart beats excitedly and I can't tell if it's because she might have seen me or that I'm looking into her eyes for the first time in so long.

She disappears into the car, and I instantly miss her eyes on me, the loneliness I've tried to ignore swelling up larger than ever. The car pulls away and I wait a few beats before I pull out a few cars behind them. They were both dressed up and that means they're going somewhere classy. Selene is not a classy female but maybe *Candy* is. I shudder at the name and instantly recoil. It's disgusting and I can't believe she chose that over her gorgeous name's meaning.

Just as I thought, I watch as the BMW pulls in front of a theater, and they both get out, Selene's eyes landing on my car again as I drive by. She's noticed my vehicle and now I need to decide my next move. Do I keep it and let her know I am indeed following her, or do I rent another and throw her off my scent? It also boils down to safety. Do I risk a knife in my throat or not?

I pull into a parking lot a few buildings down and haul out my phone, dialing Zander.

"What's happened?" he picks up, sounding frantic.

I roll my eyes and shake my head, "you sound like a little pussy."

"Yeah," he exhales, "I know. Things are getting out of hand over here and I need something."

"She's met up with John again, finally."

"Are you ready to take him down? When do you want us to come?" again he frantically throws out questions.

"I'm waiting to get a good idea on the next shipment, and I think that's the information Selene is looking for, too." I explain.

I hate having to constantly tell him each move I make but if I don't keep him up to speed, they'll show up and Santos will blow all our covers.

"I can't believe Mack is dropping off for John, too. What are the fucking chances of that?"

"It's fucking luck if you ask me," I growl, "now I can finally kill that fat, toothless fuck."

Zander grunts his agreement into the phone knowing I've more right to kill that bitch than any other.

"I think she saw me," I say quietly and Zander sucks in a breath. "Or she's noticing the car."

"Fuck," he groans, "do you think she'll run again?"

"Hell no," I scoff, "I think she'll try to kill me."

"Even if she knows it's you?" he sounds shocked.

"Even more so," I chuckle, "I left her gifts like a fucking cat leaving bird heads around, she'll gut me without thought."

"She's so fucking disturbed, it's so fucking hot." He moans and I roll my eyes, even though I agree.

"I'll call with an update in the morning." I hang up before he can pry more info out of me and scrub my hand through the scruff on my chin.

I pull up the theater on my phone and find out it's playing two Broadway Productions tonight. One that is nearly over and another that's starting in ten minutes. The duration is two hours. I pull out of the parking lot and head over to John's place. It's an assumption but I do believe he'll bring her back there, especially after seeing her place and knowing his tastes.

I drive by the bar and see the woman Selene was with a few nights ago. She's leaning against the brick and speaking to two men. She looks uncomfortable and I consider it for all of two seconds before I pull a U-turn and pull up to the curb.

"Are you free?" I call out to her, and she stares at me, probably the scar on my face putting her off. Then she looks to the two guys that were crowding her space and steps around them.

"Sure, Sugar." She walks up to the car, her purple hair looking even brighter under the streetlamp. She leans into the open window and swallows nervously, "what were you looking for?"

"Nothing actually," I shrug, "you looked uncomfortable with them crowding your space, thought I'd see if you needed help."

She looks back at the guys over her shoulder as they leer at her upturned ass, "I was uncomfortable." She looks back into my face, "but you also look like you might murder me."

"Only if you annoy the fuck out of me from here to wherever you want me to drop you off." It's the truth.

She laughs suddenly and the sound shocks both her and I, "okay, grumpy, thanks for the ride."

My heart thumps against my ribcage at her calling me Grumpy. That's what Selene used to call me in the beginning too. I pull away from the curb as the other two guys call out, both pissed off I took their entertainment.

"Aren't you afraid to be doing this job right now? With all the shit going on?" I ask her, "and where am I dropping you off?"

"It's scary but I don't have a choice." She points ahead, "see those apartment buildings? My friend lives there. I think I'll pay her a visit."

She's talking about Selene and even though I know she's not home, I can't tell her that. I drive to the apartment building and park in front, looking at her expectantly. I hate talking to people and I'm already regretting picking her up because she's not moving. The things I do for Selene.

"Is there a way I can repay you?" her voice turns raspy, and my dick begins to swell. Maybe it's because I miss my girl and I know this one sitting beside me, had a taste of her. She looks down to my lap and whistles, "he's a big boy." Her hand reaches out and I latch onto the wrist, squeezing her bones together. She whimpers and the noise has me hard as a fucking rock.

"I don't need your payment." I grit out.

"I wanted to regardless of if you did anything for me, I think you're intriguing."

No one has ever called me that, the ugly scar down my face has always scared people, and in all honesty, I like it that way. I press her hand down on top of my dick and she gasps as she grabs it through my track pants.

"Tell me what you want," she whispers, her eyes still rounded at her hand gripping my cock.

"I want you to choke on it."

She grins and pulls me out, literally purring when she sees the piercing through the top. "I wish I could have this inside me." I ignore her words because I couldn't imagine ever being inside another woman again, Selene's pussy is it for me. But I don't mind her choking on it. She flicks the piercing with her tongue, and I grunt, the sensation snaking down into my balls.

She begins a steady bobbing rhythm on my cock and it's kind of boring, it only makes me miss my crazy ass bitch more. I fist her purple curls in my hand and shove her down on my cock, her gags making my balls tighten. I savagely continue to shove her down and bring her up, her hands finding purchase on my thighs. I close my eyes and imagine it's my girl, her throat constricting as I punish her esophagus. Her nails dig into the skin of my thighs, and I moan through the sting.

With one final rough thrust, I empty myself down her throat, and she swallows rapidly. I finally release her head, and she snaps up, anger clear in her eyes. She's panting trying to catch her breath and I give her a slow taunting smile. She fucking asked for it. I unlock the car doors, the sound resounding in the small space, and wait for her to get the fuck out.

"You're crazy," she breathes, and I raise a brow, I just want her out of my car. She served her fucking purpose.

She turns on a growl and throws open the door, stepping out onto the sidewalk. Then she slams it hard behind her and I can't help the chuckle that works its way up my chest. She's a fireball too and I can see why Selene is so intrigued.

John's annoying me tonight. Everything right down to his voice is grating on all my nerves, and when he suggests we head back to his place, I have to force myself to smile and seem keen on the idea. In reality, I'm imagining all the ways I can end him when I have no use for him anymore.

He makes small talk the entire fucking drive, talking about the theatre and giving me no choice but to swoon at his bullshit. I'm already uneasy after knowing some cunt came all over my coffee table then left the albino fucker's severed dick behind, but I spotted the same car a few times tonight when I felt someone's eyes on me, and that's causing my good mood to sway towards murderous.

I hope to God John 'Dumpster' just wants a blow job and passes the fuck out like last time, because I want to barricade myself in my apartment and get my shit together. I need to be prepared in case that bastard breaks in again, I might spend the evening sharpening my knives and getting ready to go all Edward Scissor-Hands on the prick.

I need to kill someone, but I have to be extra fucking careful since there's a copycat lurking around. My thoughts stray to Santos again, confusion swirling in my brain. It's definitely something he'd do to fuck with my head, but he would have shown himself by now, wanting me to know it was him.

I miss that crazy psycho. And I miss the hell out of his devil dick and sharp blade. No one fucks like my guys.

Well, Aniyah fucks like a dream, I guess.

The car slows and I convince myself to relax, not wanting John to pick up on my mood. He'll ask questions, and if he thinks something is weird even for a second, he'll catch on that something isn't right. I can't fucking risk it.

He steps from the car and offers his hand, waiting for me to take it so he can help me step out. Knowing it's an act makes my blood boil.

How many girls did he make swoon before abusing their fucking trust? How many young women or children looked to him for safety, just to be used and broken? Fuck, I have to get hold of myself before I beat the piece of shit to a pulp and use him as compost in his own fucking garden.

"You look good enough to eat," John murmurs as we wander inside, my heels clicking on the shiny floors.

"I hope so," I giggle, fluttering my lashes and putting my placid mask back in place.

He leads me up to his room, not even offering me a drink this time before shutting the door and pressing me against it, his lips trailing down my neck with a groan.

"You smell delicious. I've hardly been able to keep my hands to myself all evening," he says against my skin, and I wish I could slam my knee into his balls.

If my stalker is killing off the men I fuck, why haven't they hacked this cunt to pieces? Surely, they've seen us together a few times. Do they have their eyes on him too? Do they know something about the missing women that I don't? I wish they'd come out of fucking hiding so I can decide if they're useful, or just another stab for my blade.

I'll stab them for sure for the fucking gifts they've left me, but their willingness to help would determine where and how deep I'll stab them.

I fake a moan as John's fingers run across my pussy from the outside of my clothes, and just before he can dip his fingers under the fabric, his phone rings loudly from his pocket.

He scowls, glancing at the screen before his face becomes serious.

"Sorry, Candy. I need to take this. One of the girls will show you out." Then he opens the door and leaves me standing there, my prayers answered.

I head back down to the front door, not bothering to snoop even though it's the perfect opportunity. I want my bed, and a quiet night.

I order an Uber and wait on the side of the road, only having to wait a few minutes. I stare out the window the entire way home, my eyes zoning in on the car that has been following me today. The windows are too tinted to see through, but I can feel their eyes on me as I step out of the Uber.

The moment I step towards my apartment, the stalker car pulls away from the curb, making me frown. Were they making sure I got home safely, or making sure I'm home alone to come back while I'm sleeping and gut me? Fucker can try.

I make my way up to my door, halting when I notice Aniyah waiting in front of it. After the day I've had, the last thing I feel like doing is making chit chat over wine. Why the fuck didn't she call before showing up?

Her eyes dart to mine as I approach, and I hate how her face lights up. She doesn't want me, but here she is, acting like I mean something to her after a long shitty day on the job.

"Hey, babe. I…"

"What are you doing here?" I cut in bluntly, her smile dropping as I nudge past her to unlock my door. Petty, I know, but she has no right fucking with my head like this.

She follows me inside without an invite, causing my teeth to grind.

"I wanted to see you. Is that a crime?" She asks lightly with a laugh, but it's forced, so I know she's picked up on my mood. Why is she still here then?

I drop my keys on the table and grab a bottle of whiskey from the shelf, not bothering with a glass as I drink straight from the bottle before answering.

"You should have called. Why'd you just show up?" I grunt, usually not caring about being a bitch, but something nags at me this time. I need her gone, mainly because of that psychopathic stalker on the loose, but also because I want to be alone.

I need to center myself again, then take on the next day's challenges with a clear head. I might even hunt down a piece of shit to let out some of my thirst for blood that I have to keep under control.

Aniyah watches me closely, her jaw clenching as she finally looks away.

"I had a shitty night and thought I could stop by to forget about it. Everyone was a dick to me, and now you're being one too."

"You're the one in my apartment. I didn't track you down. I can't fucking afford you tonight anyway," I throw back, knowing it's a cheap shot.

Anger fills her eyes for a moment before she spins on her heels and heads towards the door, speaking over the shoulder I had my teeth in last night.

"Sorry, I should have checked your fucking budget first. Fuck you."

The door slams behind her, and I drop my head back against the wall and gulp down a healthy amount of whiskey. I hope my stalker breaks in again because I'm ready to make some fucker bleed. I don't give a fuck if it's in my own fucking kitchen, either.

REAPED

Chapter Thirteen

Darius

J jerk my gaze down the bar when I hear a loud smash, not surprised to see Santos brawling with some drunken idiot. He's been trying to pick a fight with someone for hours, and it seems someone finally snapped at his antagonizing.

Zander raises an eyebrow as he joins me, watching our psycho buddy beat the shit out of the guy. "I fucking told you this was a dumb idea," he grunts, making me shrug.

"He's got some steam to let loose, he's fine."

"Fine? Dude, he's going to murder that asshole with his fucking bare hands. Get over there and break it up," he growls, turning his attention to me. He's never been the type to tolerate our bullshit, but he's worse without our girl around.

I sigh, draining my glass and standing. "Give him a few more minutes. It would be nice to get home and not get the hell kicked out of me for one night."

"If we need to lock him up…"

I glare at him, wanting to punch him in the face for even suggesting we lock Santos up. He's crazy, but he isn't a fucking animal.

I must look like I'm ready to strangle him, because he puts his hands out in front of himself.

"I'm joking but go and contain him before some cunt calls the cops. The last thing we need is that idiot getting arrested and trying to murder a whole bunch of them."

I roll my eyes at his dramatics as I move towards the fight, letting out a whistle to draw Santos' attention. He glances up, his drunken gaze connecting with mine. "C'mon, brother. Wrap this up and let's get home."

"Five more minutes?" he whines, waiting for me to nod before grabbing the guy by the front of the shirt and wailing into him again. The bartender gives me a filthy look, and I narrow my eyes on him.

"The fuck are you looking at?" I demand, his eyes widening a fraction.

"Your buddy needs to go. I can't have people fighting in my bar," he insists, jumping as I slam my palm down on the bar.

"My boy just needs a minute, then we'll be gone. Can't you see he's stressed?" I bite out, glancing at Santos who's practically laughing like a hyena suddenly.

"Take that, ye scallywag! Victory is mine!" he declares, causing a smirk to tug at my lips. He really means the world to me, the funny fucker.

The bartender glares at me, so I flip him the bird. "Yeah, yeah. I'm getting him."

I walk up to Santos, who gives me a big grin. "Did you see that, D? I fucking got him good!" he beams, dropping an arm over my shoulders to give me some of his weight. He's beyond drunk, and he's lucky Blaze isn't around to stab him. That grumpy bastard hates it when either of us gets annoyingly drunk like this.

I slide an arm around his waist, giving him more support. "How the fuck can you fight when you can hardly walk?"

"Just like how I manage to dick someone down when I'm drunk. Superpowers and whiskey!" He exclaims, Zander shakes his head and chuckles as he walks up to us.

Santos suddenly yanks back, almost stumbling over like a rag doll. "Hey! Take a fucking photo, asswipe!" he barks at the bartender, staggering towards the bar.

"Dammit, Darius," Zander growls, but I motion towards the bartender and shrug.

"What? I said to that fucker we were going. It's not my fault he looked at Santos."

Santos bickers with the dickhead for a while, before grabbing a bar stool and smashing it against the bar, sending pieces of wood flying.

"Avast ye! Ye lily-livered sea bass!"

"What the fuck did he just say?" Zander snorts.

"He said pay attention, then insulted him. It's like the polite version of a cunt, I guess," I reply, sensing his eyes landing on me.

"You actually understand that gibberish?"

"Gibberish? It's pirate," I gasp, acting offended and earning an eye roll. I'd die for Zander, but our relationship is different to the one Santos and I share.

"Does ye want to dance the hempen jig?!"

Zander glances at me and waits, making me sigh. Pirate isn't that hard to interpret, compared to all the other shit Santos says on the regular.

"He threatened to hang him."

"Where the fuck do you two learn this shit?" he scoffs, a laugh leaving me.

"Google. We get bored sometimes."

Santos manages to scramble onto the bar, holding a broken bar stool leg in his grip as he waves it at the bartender who doesn't seem to know what to do.

"En garde! Shark bait!" he screams, and I interpret as he goes.

"You can figure out en garde, and shark bait basically means he's gonna die."

Zander is sniggering as we watch our brother, and it's the most fun we've had in ages, I swear. Just when I think he's calming down, he throws his make-shift sword, knocking bottles off the shelf in the process. "I'll make ye walk the plank!"

"Get him out of here, they're going to call the cops," Zander laughs as Santos snatches a bottle of whiskey and starts chugging it. I finally move up to the bar and grab him by the legs, tugging him back and managing to catch him before he breaks his neck.

"You're three sheets to the wind, matey," I chuckle, starting to drag him towards the door before he gets any more ideas on his attack. I try to wrestle the whiskey out of his hands, but he fights me on it.

"Hands off me booty!" he slurs, laughter bubbling up before I can stop it.

"I'll put my hands on your booty whenever I want."

"Wait! We can't go yet, I have to blow the man down!" he argues, but he gets nowhere as Zander takes up his other side to help me.

"Why do you need to do that?" Zander grins, "Because dead men tell no tales?"

Santos stops fighting me and stares at him, his eyes going wide. "I didn't know you spoke pirate too!"

By the time we manage to get him into the car and get the whiskey away from him, our stomachs are hurting from laughing so hard. Santos falls into the back seat, cursing as he smacks his head on the car door. "Son of a biscuit eater!"

I'm laughing so fucking hard I swear I'm going to piss my pants, and Zander's fighting to contain his too as he slides into the driver's seat. I sit in the back with Santos, helping him sit up straighter so I can buckle him in.

"You're lucky Blaze isn't here, because he would have fucking stabbed you tonight," I inform him, making him snort.

"He loves me! Why would that asshole stab me?"

Zander starts the car, peering over his shoulder at Santos with a smirk. "Because Blaze is daddy."

"Well, he can suck on my cackle fruit," he mumbles, and I hoot with laughter.

"Your chicken eggs?"

"Shit, that's not right," he mutters to himself, trying to remember the right term.

The drive home is full of him complaining that he didn't get to kill anyone, and it takes both Zander and I to carry the drunk bastard up to his room. Zander brings a bucket in to sit beside the bed, then leaves me to undress Santos and tuck him in, saying goodnight and knowing I'll be sleeping in here with him.

I strip down to my boxers, then manage to pull Santos' shirt over his head before reaching for his belt, making a low chuckle leave him as he lies on his back with his eyes shut.

"You're not even going to buy me dinner first?"

"I think we're past that, don't you?" I tease, unbuckling the belt and loosening his pants to tug them down his legs. I help him into bed properly once he's in nothing but his boxers, and I'm surprised when his hand darts out to grab the back of my neck, dragging me down to kiss him.

His hand lets go once he knows I won't pull back, and he slides it down my bare back, pulling my body closer. He's way too drunk to get hard, I know that much, but as his tongue glides against mine, something calms in my chest.

It's been hard without Selene, and our emotions are all over the place without her, but this? This is what we need. The comfort that only we can bring to each other. I know Santos will never leave me, but he hasn't let me wander far from his sight since she left us, probably worried that maybe I'll abandon him too.

Santos is a crazy bastard, but he gives his everything for those he loves.

I groan as his hand slips into the back of my boxers and his palm squeezes my butt cheek, his leg going over mine to keep me close.

When I finally pull back, we're both panting, and Santos' eyes appear calm for the first time in days. He needs me to calm his demons, and I'll always do that for him.

"I love you, D," he murmurs, his eyes flicking between mine. He needs to feel wanted, and I'll gladly give him that.

I curl against him, nuzzling into his neck and running my hand over his abs.

"Love you too, San. Get some sleep, I'll be here when you wake up," I promise, knowing it's the right thing to say, because within seconds his breathing evens out and he is asleep.

I wake up to the sound of retching, knowing Santos' big night is back to bite him in the ass. I lie in bed for a while before moving. Darius will be looking after him and I'm not needed.

It's weird not having Blaze around to maintain control, and I miss that grumpy prick something fierce, but I must admit, it was funny watching Santos last night. I have no idea how Darius keeps up with him, but they're two peas in a pod and I can't imagine them being without each other.

I chuckle as I think back to Santos on the bar, waving his fake sword around. That fucker is crazy, and as much as he drives Blaze and I mental regularly, I wouldn't have him any other way.

I finally climb from the bed and pad down the hallway, peeking into the bathroom to find Santos sitting in front of the toilet with his head in it, while Darius sits back and runs a hand up and down his spine.

Santos violently heaves, and I wince at knowing how his stomach will feel later if he's heaving like that for long.

I step inside and lean against the wall, meeting Darius' gaze as he notices me. "Morning. How's the Captain this morning?"

Santos throws up again, a groan of pain leaving him. "Pretty sure Davy Jones' locker is awaiting me," he manages to get out, making me smirk.

"Learned your lesson then?"

"Fuck no," he mumbles and leans back, getting comfortable between Darius' legs and pressing his back against his chest to close his eyes.

"So, what's on the agenda for today?" I ask, managing not to snigger when Santos replies.

"Death."

Darius absently presses a kiss to his shoulder, and it takes a second for me to process it. They share a bond between them that's different from what they share with Blaze and me.

They've never labelled what they are, just going with what feels right and having each other's backs.

"Day at home then?" I offer, and Santos nods, wincing with the movement.

"Yeah. Maybe in a few hours we can put a movie on or something. We can just hang out," he answers, shivering slightly from the cold.

"How about you two get off the cold floor and get dressed. Actually, scratch that. Get Santos in the shower. He smells like stale whiskey," I retort, causing Santos to groan and lean forward to throw up again.

Darius manages to get him to his feet, stepping into the shower with him to help hold him up. These two are pros at writing themselves off, so I leave them to it and head into the kitchen, knowing everyone will be needing some fucking coffee.

Selene

I haven't heard from Aniyah in a few days and to be honest, that's a good thing. This is what I wanted right? To push her away and keep her safe. I've been staying away from the bar because I haven't wanted to see her and spent the last few nights on the other side of town speaking to a group of girls. Girls are going missing all over Nevada and the news outlets haven't been reporting it. What's a few missing hookers anyway?

I can see the fear in their faces and it's wrenching my heart right out of my chest. They have no other choice but to come out here every night and face their demons, their fears having to be pushed to the back burner. How else will they survive when this is all they've ever known?

"Have you felt anything weird about a certain client?" I question one girl who looks no older than eighteen. "Maybe he was new around here?"

"They're all new," another girl chimes in, "they come here to get away from their wives, gamble some money, and fuck a few whores."

"I hear you." I nod, "listen to your instincts, we have them more than others, and don't get in a car with anyone looking suss." I can't warn them anymore and if they at least know something weird is going down, maybe it'll make them more cautious.

"There was one rich motherfucker the other night, he said he was having a party." A girl with long bleached blonde hair says as she strides up to me. She looks a bit like myself, "he said he wanted me to come and offered me ten grand."

Another girl whistles and I raise a brow, "why didn't you go?"

"Because ten grand is way too much for just a simple party, I knew I was either getting gang raped or snatched. No one should have to entice a hooker with a large number. Most of the time they're trying to fight our prices down." She's not wrong.

"That's smart," I smile at her. I know many girls who would've run for that money without a single thought.

"Just because we sell our pussies, doesn't mean we're dumb." She retorts and gives me a once over. My trench is done up and my hair in a messy bun on top of my head. Looking at me I guess it wouldn't look like I work the same damn job she does.

"Don't I know it, sweetheart," I step closer to her, "I think we're smarter because of it."

Her eyes widen with my admission, and I turn away from her, no longer wanting to carry on the conversation. I walk down the street, my strides wide, and scan all the cars on the side of the road. I haven't seen the black sedan with the dark tinted windows in a few days, but that doesn't mean I'm not being followed. I can still sense it and I can't shake the feeling that this person knows where I came from.

I was hoping for a while that it was one of my boys, that they cared enough to follow me here, and wanted to keep me safe while I searched for my sister. I no longer think it's them. They would've shown themselves by now for sure. Especially seeing as someone dumped a fucking sausage on my counter.

Fifteen minutes later and I'm standing in front of Good Times. I haven't been here for a few days and right now I'm longing for the few friends I've made here. My life has been a slideshow of loneliness and the guys showed me what it was like to have someone, now I crave it.

I step through the doors and see it's a bit livelier than usual, the music a few notches louder. I go to my stool and find a female sitting in it, twirling her red hair around her finger.

"You're in her seat." Colleen appears telling the girl I'm staring at.

She turns to look at me with a look of disgust until she takes in my appearance. I don't look like a sugar Candy sweetheart today, I'm in all black, and my makeup is dark. I watch her swallow visibly then slide off the stool, hurrying to the other end of the bar.

I sit in my stool and a whiskey on the rocks slides in front of me. "Been a while." Colleen tsks and I look up at her.

"Just busy." I shrug, "I was checking in."

"I know," she leans on the bar, "it's just been boring here without you."

I gulp down the amber liquid and welcome the familiar burn as it skates down my throat. I haven't looked around the bar for purple curls yet and I don't know why, I've clearly become a pussy.

"How's Aniyah been?" I look into Colleen's eyes.

"She hasn't been with you?" I watch as worry saturates her features, and my heart begins to pound.

"No," I straighten, "why the fuck would you think she was with me?"

"I saw you two leave together and you've both been MIA these last few days…" she trails off, horror filling her eyes. "No."

"She was at my apartment a few days ago, but I haven't seen her since then." I stand abruptly and the stool tips over behind me. I remember Aniyah telling me about a date she had scheduled with John and my mouth instantly goes dry.

Why would he take her now? It's makes no fucking sense. I run out of the bar, and I hear Colleen calling out to me, but I can't waste any more time. I run down the sidewalk and toward my building, praying that she'll be there. What if the person that was stalking me decided to snatch her? What if I find a body part of hers in my house? My heart feels like it's pushing up through my throat and I'm taken back to when I first lost Jan.

I rush inside and when I get to my floor, my heart sinks further when I don't find her waiting there. I throw open my apartment door and stalk inside. I look through each room and when it turns up empty, I'm both relieved and scared. I pull out my burner phone and fire a text off to John, I think it's time for him and me to really get together. I really hate that I didn't take the opportunity to snoop when I had the chance, but I can't do anything about it now.

He messages me back, sounding smug that I'm so eager to see him, but says for me to come by his place. This is it, my chance to really find out what I can about John and hopefully find Aniyah in the process. I can only hope she's off sulking somewhere about our last exchange, but I know she's not, she was only interested in sex with me, and she wouldn't be sulking, she's pissed.

I pull on a bright pink sweater and a light blue jean skirt, pulling my hair back into a high ponytail. I make sure to strap my belt around my waist and then I call an Uber to pick me up. It's time to get the answers I've been pussy footing around for and if I have to spill John's guts on the floor tonight, so fucking be it.

I step to the curb just as the Uber pulls up and my eyes focus over the top of the car, landing on an all-black sedan idling across the street. I can't see the driver but for some reason I want them to know I see them, and I want them to follow me. Even if it's my stalker, I want at least one person to know where I am, and that makes me feel like maybe I'm not so alone.

When John's house comes into view, I feel a cold chill slip down the nape of my neck, and I sense an evil I've never felt any other time I've been here. Something's different or fuck, maybe I'm just different but tonight changes everything. There's no more Miss Nice Selene. I get out of the car and hear another idling not too far behind, causing me to pause. That tingle on my neck is strong and I know without looking just what car is sitting down the street.

I walk up the driveway and notice the garage door is only halfway shut, like the motor got stuck or something is blocking the sensor. I can see the BMW's bumper in there and I brush it off as I step up to the porch. I ring the doorbell and John appears a few seconds later in an unbuttoned dress shirt and grey slacks.

"I was surprised when I got your message-"

"Cut the shit, John," I cut him off and step into the house slamming the door behind me. His brows raise at my tone and use of language. "You're going to fuck me and you're going to do it now."

I fist his sweater and haul him in, watching as his eyes darken with lust. He licks his lips and grins as he grabs my hair in his hand, yanking my head back forcefully. There you are, you little prick.

"I really like this side of you, Candy." He growls before sucking on the skin of my neck, "this makes me want to do things to you I shouldn't."

"Nothing's off the table, John." I fist his hair in my hand and yank him off my neck, "just stop toying with me. It makes you sound like a fucking pussy."

His growl is the only warning I get before I'm forcefully turned around and shoved into the wall, his hand gripping the back of my neck. Here we go. He flips up my skirt and slaps my ass, hard. I moan at the contact and Blaze is here clear in my mind. I can get through this if I imagine it's him. His rough hands slapping down on my tender flesh and scruffy chin digging into my neck.

My hand slides down the wall and lands on a door handle. I press down on the lever since I'm supposed to be scoping the place out, and the door opens into the garage. I see the BMW and a large steel trapdoor on the floor before John reaches out, pulling it shut.

"Sorry," I whisper, and he goes right back to slapping my ass. Worst shit ever, I can't even imagine Blaze because he would be so much better than this.

I wonder what's under that trapdoor, nothing good ever sits beneath a trapdoor, and I have a feeling that's where I need to go look. John latches onto my thong and rips it off my body, the fabric burning my skin with the force. I hiss through the sting, and he chuckles, giving me another slap on the ass. I can't wait until he's bleeding out and then I will slap the shit out of his fucking ass. He jams a finger up inside me and I bite my tongue to hold in my snarl. I can get through this and then I'm going to use my pussy power to make him tell me what's in that garage.

I feel the tip of his cock press against my barely wet pussy when his phone rings.

"Do not answer that," I sound more aggressive than I mean to.

"I…" I can hear him debating inside his pea brain and roll my eyes.

"I can come back tomorrow." I huff and yank down my skirt. I turn to look at him and he's stuffing himself back in his pants.

"Yes," he begins to pull his phone out, "thank you, Candy."

I pull out my phone, seemingly to call an Uber, and step outside. I'm happy his cock never got the chance to sink into me. I step down onto the driveway and look at the garage door, a smile creeps along my mouth. I forgot this thing was left halfway open. I bend down and look inside, seeing the door still shut to the house. I crawl under the door and stand up inside, making my way to the trapdoor.

I run my foot across the gleaming metal and tap it lightly. It sounds solid and what other reason would this be here but for a nefarious one? Who has a trapdoor in their house to store anything but skin? This must be where he keeps the people he *traps,* and this must be where Aniyah is. I bend to get a better look and see a large industrial latch, with a large industrial padlock. *Fuck.*

It's a newer one that has a rotary set of four numbers on the front. Four numbers from zero to nine and I don't have the slightest clue what they could be. I can't break it open because that would be too noisy and sitting here trying to figure out a combination of numbers is impossible. I let out a small groan and lean back against his fucking car, the license plate digging into my back. I turn to move away from it when the numbers literally flash in my vision.

8818.

It can't be, would he be so fucking stupid? I grab the padlock in my hand and rotate the numbers to match the license plate. I take a deep breath and pull it, watching as the bar pops open at the top. I fucking love how stupid some criminals can be, it really works in my favor. I pull open the door and look down at a steep descending staircase. I rest the heavy door against the garage wall and begin my way down, it's dark save for the square of light coming from the doorway. I step to the bottom of the stairs and look ahead into a blackened abyss, there's no light at the other end.

I hear hinges creak above me and look up quickly, startled by the noise. Standing at the opening is John and his smile is wide. "This saves me a lot of trouble, Candy. I'm glad you found your own way down there."

"What is this place, John?" I ask, no longer acting like the sweet little prostitute.

He smiles maniacally and closes the door, "have fun in the dark, Candy."

If he wants me to scream, then he is barking up the wrong bitch. I pull my phone out and see there's no reception, not that I need any, I have no one to call. The little light from the screen is what I really want, and I shine it ahead of me. I see another set of stairs about twenty feet away and head towards them, where else can I go? The floor is concrete as are the walls and ceiling, all fortified and tough. It would have to be to withstand being underground. I get to the stairs and see another door above. I hope that one's unlocked because if not, I'll end up dying down here.

I begin to climb the stairs, closing my phone and popping it back in my pocket. I get to the door and give it a shove, thankful when it opens. I pop my head out and groan when I see what's in front of me.

Chapter Fourteen

Blaze

She went into that garage and never came back out. I don't know what she found in there, but I can bet she's trapped, either of her own making or by John. Now I'm at a loss of how to proceed, do I head in there and possibly fuck everything up for her? Or do I watch everything closely and follow like the dog I am right now? I feel like a watchdog, and I just want to sink my teeth into some perverted flesh and watch them bleed out.

A few hours later and still no movement from the house, so I call up the boys. I think it's time we crash her party, Selene doesn't seem to be getting any further in her search, and I haven't seen her come out of this damn house. I can see the sun beginning to set and I have a bad feeling. I pull out my phone and call Zander.

"Blaze." He always picks up the phone sounding anxious, I bet those two idiots are driving him mental.

"Pack your bags and get your asses here. I'm sending you the address and I'll need you on the red eye."

"Santos!" he screams into the phone, and I fist my hand. "We're going to get our girl!"

"Finally! I already packed our bags when she took off, let's gooooo!" I hear his voice in the background.

"He sounds a bit off." I remark.

"You don't understand how bad we need to do this." Zander sounds tired.

"Sleep on the plane and hurry the fuck up." I hang up the phone and send them John's address. Now I wait.

I hear an engine coming up the street and sit up in my seat. It's Delaney's van and when he pulls into the driveway my heart nearly falls out of my ass. He's here for a pickup and my fucking girl is in there. I can't take them both on and make sure the girls are kept safe. I don't even know how to get to them. I look at the dash and huff, still another half an hour until they arrive. They've landed but driving here will take time.

We have some time because I know they won't load the girls until well into the night and then they'll have to wait until the street grows quiet. Time moves slowly and so do my fucking friends; they should be here by now. Who the fuck is driving? Darius? He's the fucking grandpa out of us behind the wheel. Santos is never allowed to drive because he thinks it's funny to 'nudge' people out of the way with his bumper.

The BMW is pulled out of the garage and the van backs into the space, readying for a pickup. I slam my fist to the wheel knowing there's not much I can do, and I just pray that John will divulge all he knows as he stares down the edge of my blade. I try to get a good look inside the garage, but it's no use, and it fuels my anger even more. Wouldn't Selene put up a fight? Unless she's wanting to be loaded up like cattle.

It takes all of ten minutes this time and the van is once again leaving the driveway, the windows black. It's impossible to tell if she's in there. I slam my fist into the steering wheel a couple more times and hold onto the guilt I'm feeling for letting this happen. I'll need it to gut our new friend John.

Five minutes later, Zander pulls up and drives by the house slowly, pulling up to park behind me. I stay in the driver's seat and watch as they all get out. Zander looks tired but his eyes are filled with fury. Darius looks cautious and his body is tight with tension. Then there's Santos. He's hopping out of the damn vehicle like he's about to watch the circus, his smile stretching wide across his face. Crazy fucker.

I open the door and step out, cracking my stiff neck. Zander approaches cautiously and lays a hand on my shoulder.

"Brother," he squeezes. "How are you doing?"

"No slips." I assure him, "until now."

I can feel the rage swooping in and I'm about to lose myself to it. He sees the moment I vibrate and turns to the guys.

"Let's get inside and bleed this fucker out."

Santos hoots and pulls out a blade, checking the sharpness of the edge. Darius is rubbing his hands together, all too excited to cause some mayhem. So the fuck am I.

"I don't know if she's still in there, Mack was by earlier for a pickup." I tell them.

"But that little pussy bitch is still inside, right?" Santos grins, "the one that's been dating our girl?"

"Yeah," I nod.

"Then let's go find out where she is." Zander starts for the driveway, the rest of us following behind.

I let him lead because I'd rather protect my brother's backs, they need me, and I would never let anything happen to them. Zander rings the doorbell while Santos smooths down his shirt, like he's meeting the fucking president. I stand up beside them and the four of us have the fucking porch crowded. John would be smart not to open the door, not that that would stop us.

He is a dumb fuck it seems, since the door opens, and his eyes widen as he looks between us.

"Can I help you?" his voice cracks.

"We are Girl Guides, and we have a bag of cookies for you to buy." Santos cuts in and causes the other two to snicker.

I push through them and then I'm shoving John back, my anger now fully in control.

"You have something that belongs to me and I'm gonna need it back." My spit flies on his face. Like most people, he takes in the scar on my face, and swallows thickly in fear.

"I think you're mistaken; I have nothing here." He is fucking shaking under my grip.

The guys enter the house after me, kicking the door shut behind them.

"Let's go to the garage." I say and watch as his eyes widen.

I shove him hard and his hand shakes as he reaches for the door handle.

"What's in the garage?" I hear Santos ask behind me. "Better not be my sex kitten."

I watch as John walks over to the large steel trap door in the center of the garage and breathes out a large breath. "Open it." I demand.

He puts the combination into the lock and then he's hefting the large door, revealing a narrow staircase. We all stand around and peer down at the pitch black.

"Let's go." I grab John's collar and shove him forward.

Zander pulls out his phone and turns on the flashlight app, illuminating the steps. There's about ten of them and then nothing but a tunnel. It makes me angry thinking Selene is down there or was down there. John takes a shaky step down into the hole, stretching his hand out to the wall for stability.

"They're not here." He says quietly and I crack my teeth together.

"Where are they?" I demand stepping down behind him.

"With their buyer by now."

"Well, you're going to show me where you keep them regardless." I shove him and he stumbles down the last few stairs.

We hit the ground and I growl as we walk in darkness to another set of stairs, it smells like a horse stable. Of course, the girls weren't cared for while here and the smell is evidence enough. He starts up the next set of stairs and opens the door above our heads.

"Oh fuck, it stinks." Darius covers his nose.

It has a strong scent of urine, and even I crinkle my nose at the scent. I shove John upward and into what I know is the small structure that's located in his backyard. We all come up behind him and look into a room that has a few chairs. There are a few buckets in the corners that I gather are filled with piss.

"See, nothing here." He holds out his arms and Darius springs forward, smacking him in the face like the bitch he is.

"Where is Selene?" he screams.

"I don't know who that is." John begins to shake as we all crowd around him.

"Tall blonde with nice tits." Santos elaborates and Zander snorts.

"Candy?" John asks and I punch him in the gut.

"She is sweet as candy but only when she's sleeping." Zander snickers.

"Where are the girls?" I ask John and shove him down into a chair.

"I sold them." He licks his lips and Zander pulls out a gun. "Okay," he holds up his hands. "I can tell you to whom."

"You better make it fast, that girl is really special." Zander growls.

"To an MC in northern Nevada. They call themselves Dientes Afilados."

"Sharp Teeth?" Santos mutters and looks unconvinced.

"Yes, they are in McDermitt." John nods profusely. "I will give you a cut of what I made if you'll just let me go back to the house."

"How do you know Mack Delaney?" I ask him and his eyebrows shoot up.

"Him and I met through mutual business partners."

"Enough talking, time for blood." Darius steps forward and Santos follows with his blade.

If I don't reel myself in a little, I'm going to kill this fucker too fast. I need the cunt to suffer for putting his hands on our girl, even if she allowed it.

Darius grins as he moves around behind the guy, giving me an amused glance. "What do you think, brother? Should we start cutting off the body parts that touched our girl?"

I laugh, the loud sound bouncing off the solid walls and causing John to startle.

"I think that's a fucking excellent plan. Hey, John. How many times did you touch my fucking queen?" I ask as I circle him, a whimpering sound spilling from him as he opens his mouth to speak.

"I didn't know she had a boyfriend! She came to me, I didn't chase her!" he insists, letting out a girly scream as Darius grabs his biceps from behind and shoves him down into a chair.

"I haven't even fucking started yet! Why're you squealing like a little piggy?" I exclaim, not looking away as someone dangles a rope in front of me. I take it, wrapping it around John's legs and the chair, making sure he can't kick me before I squat in front of him, inspecting my knife.

I know Darius will keep his top half in the chair, so I take my merry fucking time. I check my teeth in the reflection, suddenly jerking forward to stab the blade right into the top of John's thigh.

He screams bloody murder, but there's no use. He built this place to block out the screams and cries of all the women he takes, so no one will be coming to save him from us.

"Where are your balls, dude? My girl doesn't even bat an eye when a blade's sliding through her soft skin. Man up a little, would you?" I tsk, eyeing him like a shark. There are so many things I want to do to this piece of shit, but I need to draw it out and make sure he doesn't die until we want him to.

I snatch his arm and hold his wrist firmly, feeling the bones shift under the pressure. Not enough to break, but enough to cause discomfort.

"Eenie, meenie, miney, mo," I laugh maniacally as I point to each finger on his hand before stopping at mo, forcing his palm down onto the arm of the chair with a sadistic grin. "Yo, one of you boys wanna give me a lighter?"

John's eyes go wide, but Zander approaches me instantly, holding his lighter out and flicking the gas, sparking the flame to life. He knows what I'm up to, they've all seen my party tricks many times.

Blaze silently pulls a blade from his pocket and holds it over the flame, earning a big smile of approval from me.

"You're turning me on, brother."

"I'll turn you off in a second with my fist," he says flatly, apparently not in the mood. Nothing new there.

I shrug, not bothered by his asshole behavior.

"You're going to brand me?" John gasps, but Darius smacks him in the back of the head sharply.

"No talking unless spoken to," he orders, my dick twitching at his tone.

I grip John's hand harder against the arm of the chair, giving the asshole a wide grin.

"I'll talk to you, Johnny boy. The answer is no. I won't waste time branding you."

Relief swims in his eyes, but he screams as my knife slams down on his finger, severing it completely. "I need to cauterize the wound though, so you don't go bleeding out on me. Playtime with Santos is fun, right?"

His screaming is music to my ears, the sound vibrating through me and calming the demons in me a little. He isn't going to live after touching my girl, and he sure as fuck isn't going to die quickly.

Blaze hands the hot blade to me, a content sigh leaving me as I press it against the bleeding stub, the smell of burning flesh filling my nose. Just as John starts to pass out from the pain, Darius tuts and shakes him awake.

"Hey! Wake up, fuckbag! You're a terrible fucking host!" he barks.

John jolts and screams again, making me groan.

"I really wish you didn't have to suffer, John, trust me. But I can't let you escape your sins so easily. You should be grateful it's us that gets to kill you. If Selene had, you'd be mutilated in ways you can't even begin to imagine. You know the Reaper Incarnate?" I whisper in his ear as I stand and move behind him.

"She…"

"Our girl is a woman of many talents. She can turn you to a pile of jelly in seconds, right? You should see what she can do with a blade. It's hotter than anything she would have done to your dick. My baby's a silent assassin, and you would have been at the top of her list," I chuckle, fisting his hair and yanking his head back to expose his throat. As tempting as it is to slide the sharp point of my blade across it, I restrain myself and release him, enjoying the scare tactic more than I should.

We repeat the finger process until I've removed four, leaving just his thumb on that hand. "Did you ever press that thumb against my girl's clit and make her feel good?"

His head is drooping, and Zander scruffs his hair and yanks him back to look up at me.

"Answer him!"

"No," he slurs, blinking rapidly to try and stay awake.

I prowl closer, rubbing my dick through my pants as I watch the fear leap into his eyes. I wish my baby were here so we could fuck on John's body when we were done. It would have been almost poetic, I think.

"So, you *didn't* treat her right?" I demand, stabbing the blade into his unharmed thigh.

The sounds leaving him aren't enough, and I motion to Blaze with a smirk. "Come on, brother. I know you want to play too."

The monster inside him is rearing to be released, I can see it a mile away. It's a mirror of my own, after all.

Blaze

"Come on, brother. I know you want to play too." Santos' words rip through my ears and lights something dark and dangerous deep inside.

It's been lonely without them and even though they make me want to bury them on a daily basis, they're my brothers. I wouldn't be where I am without them, and I will never be able to make it on my own. They keep me grounded and at times like this, let me release the beast.

When I step forward, Santos begins to grin maniacally, and he knows this is where things start to get really messy.

"I grew up in a place that treated children and young adults as cattle. Bought and bartered like prized meat, auctioned when the features were exceptionally good." I bend down into his groggy face, "I don't like what you're a part of and for that, I have to make an example out of you."

I pull the small hatchet I have from the belt around my waist and spin it in my hand. "The Vikings had amazing torture techniques and the devil I was placed with growing up loved to demonstrate some of them. The one I was most interested in unfortunately, I never got to see in real life. But I want to give it a try, nonetheless. You'll probably die before the good part but at least me and my brothers can enjoy it."

Santos hoots and Darius has a wide smile, his teeth looking large and ominous. Zander gets a certain excited look in his eyes, and I know they will remember this for the rest of their lives.

"Get him on his knees and I'll remove the shirt."

Santos and Darius jump to my command, grabbing John. They put him on his knees, and he begins to weakly plead for his life. He sounds like a fucking infant and that pisses me off, he sure acted like a grown man when he was trapping women. I grab my knife and cut the shirt down the center of his back, watching as it falls open and hangs from his arms. I can hear him begin to sob and the sound is like a dying animal, one I need to put out of its misery.

I remember every detail about what I read on this technique and my blood pumps with the chance to use it. I take my sharpened knife and slice through the skin on his back, digging down past the muscle. The blood pours out and over my hands, making the procedure messy. You're never prepared for the mess because the blood isn't depicted in any photos and it's a fucking hindrance. The slippery feel of it and then the twitching of muscles while the participant screams. It's not easy to be precise this way and it takes away from some of its beauty.

"Fuck, that's pretty." Santos coos.

It is pretty, I agree. I begin to rip the muscle from his ribs and John slumps over, hitting the chair in front of him. He lasted longer than I thought, and I don't know if he's dead or on the brink, but it doesn't matter. I want to leave a beautiful masterpiece for any of his partners that may come looking for him. Something to remember him by and a silent threat that will follow them around.

I grab my hatchet and start chopping into the ribs, breaking them open one by one. I hear Zander heave from behind me and roll my eyes, he was always the weaker one when it came to torture. He prefers his kills to be quick.

Once the ribs are cut, I begin to pry them open, pulling them outward and revealing the lungs. Beautifully red and delicate, the tissue is like the thinnest sponge. I run my fingers along the soft surface and smile as it flutters beneath my touch. The human body is an amazing thing, and the intelligence of each organ is astounding. I grip each lung in my hands and lift them out carefully, placing them over the ribs. They look like soft, red wings.

"That's beautiful." Darius whispers with awe.

We all stand in a line and stare down at the masterpiece before us, almost reverently. My hands drip with blood, my clothes are saturated with it, and my head is once again cleared.

"What is this?" Santos asks.

"The Blood Eagle."

REAPED

HUNTING THE REAPER

Chapter Fifteen

Selene

The van tips as it rounds a sharp turn and I plummet into a few of the girls.

"Son of a bitch!" I scream and bang on the van's door.

"Just sit down, Selene." Aniyah says from the corner. She looks sick, or hungry, or fucking both. Most of these girls do.

I heard the name of the driver when John carted us out like cattle, Delaney. The last name on my list and even though I'm not where I want to be, I'm closer than ever to the answers I seek. I even gave John a quick kiss goodbye on the cheek, promising I would be back, and telling him to be prepared. He laughed it off not knowing who I am, but he will soon enough, and I will reap his soul for the Devil himself.

I sit down beside Aniyah, and she drops her head to my shoulder, her breaths coming out labored. She had been held inside that room for four days with a bucket to piss in and another to drink filthy water out of. She's starving and dehydrated. She told me John must've drugged her because the last thing she remembered was sitting and watching a movie with him. Then she woke up in the room with four other girls. One of which is the same prostitute that tried to convince me she was too smart to be caught. I haven't said I told you so to her but there's still time.

"Did you know John was the man snatching up the women?" Aniyah asks quietly. She's asked me this three times now and it's beginning to worry me that she's not retaining any information.

"Yes," I tell her and run my hand over her limp curls. "That's why when I found out you were missing, I went to him to find you."

"Thank you," she whispers, and I know it's only a matter of time until she's asking me the same questions all over again.

"Where are we going?" One of the girls whimpers and I tamper down the need to snap at her. Like be strong, stand up for yourself, and be prepared to fight.

"Doesn't matter," I finger my belt, "once I get the chance, I'm gutting them all."

The smooth ride turns bumpy, and I can tell we're on gravel, a dirt road in the middle of nowhere sounds like a death sentence. The only thing stopping me from breaking loose is the fact that I know we're too valuable to be killed. The van stops and a few girls gasp in fear while I stand to face the door. I will be the first person they see and if they try anything, the fucking last as well.

The doors open to show Delaney and his gap-toothed smile, his obese gut hanging out of his shirt. He's sweating profusely in the Nevada heat and his milky yellow eyes look like the fucker might have jaundice. I look beyond him and see another van idling, two mean looking fuckers standing to the side with their arms crossed over their chests. Beyond them, it's a desert wasteland, and the heat waves off the sand.

"Let's go ladies, off to your forever homes." Delaney reaches in to grab my wrist, but I snap my leg out and kick him in the face, probably freeing his gums of a few more rotting teeth. "Fuck!" He screams as he tries to sit up, looking like a beached whale, and grabbing his mouth.

I jump down from the van and suddenly the two big, tattooed, muscled men pull out guns, training them on my face. I could throw my knife and kill one but then that other one would shoot me for sure. I need to protect the girls.

"We won't hurt you." One calls out and takes a step forward. I swear that's what every fucking serial killer ever says, I should know, I am one.

"Who are you?" I call out, giving Delaney another good kick in the head when he finally sits up, and I laugh when he's flat out once again.

"Dientes Afilado." One calls out, "do you know who we are?"

"No, I don't speak French." I huff with my hands on my hips.

They begin to chuckle and the same one motions to the van behind me, "we paid for all of them, I promise no one will get harmed. Can you please get into the van?" he motions to the vehicle behind him where I see a cooler. "We have some fruit in there and water." My parched throat clenches at the mention of water and I know I can't deprive them of that.

I go back to the van, giving Delaney another shot to the gut, and I can hear the guys still chuckling behind me. I grab the few girls that can walk and help them down from the van, watching closely as they approach the guys. They keep to their word and hand them each a bottle of water. I hoist Aniyah up and wrap her hand around my neck, putting her down gently.

One of the guys approaches us slowly, his gun down by his side, and his hand reaching out to us. "Can I help you? What's wrong with her?"

"They weren't fed or given clean water, I'm sure she's sick." I snap and he wraps his arm around Aniyah's waist.

"Okay, we'll make sure she's okay." He gives me a tight nod, "I'll need you in the back while she comes up front with us. We'll drop her off at Medical."

"Medical? Like a hospital?" I question.

"No, we have a doctor on site. You'll all get checked out eventually."

I don't like the sound of it, but I don't have any other choice and Aniyah needs the help. I give him a nod and hop up into the back of yet another van to be carted off to yet another place unknown. The girls are shoving mango in their mouths and gulping water, but I refuse to let my guard down. Yes, this feels better than John's holding facility and then Delaney's van, but we're still being treated like purchased property.

I can't tell how long we're in the van for, I've lost all sense of time, and I can't even decipher how many days it's been since I was taken. The van stops and when the back doors open, it's dusk. I let everyone else out before me and I see one of the guys standing at the door.

"Where's my friend?" I ask him and he jerks his chin behind me. I turn to see the other guy holding Aniyah and taking her into a building. "What're your names?"

He raises his brow, "I'm Bank and he's Coin."

"I see what you did there, like Coin in the Bank. Is Coin in you often?"

He lets out a startled cackle and shakes his head, a blush running along his cheeks.

"Don't worry," I shrug, "two of my guys like to fool around too and it gets me hot to watch."

"*Two* of your guys?" his grin stays firmly on his face.

"Yes, I have four."

He shuts the van's doors behind me and leads me to the building the other girls disappeared into. "Where are they then? How'd you wind up on the market?"

"I left them behind," I try to sound nonchalant as my heart breaks over the words. "I need to find my sister; she was stolen many years ago."

"What's her name?"

"Janelle." I look at him, hoping to see recognition at the name.

"Nope," he shakes his head, "I don't know a Janelle around here."

He sees my shoulders slump with his answer, "sorry."

I follow him inside and see that it's a small building with multiple bedrooms. "You'll stay here until Digs comes by." He tells me.

"Digs?"

"That's our Doc, we call him Digs because he digs out bullets on the regular." He chuckles and I decide I like the sound.

"Oh, yeah." I nod, "that makes all the sense. Where are we?"

"You're in McDermitt, it's an old, abandoned town in North Nevada. We run the MC here called Dientes Afilados, *Spanish* for Sharp Teeth."

"Why Sharp Teeth?" I scrunch my nose at the name.

"We like to bite." He snaps at me playfully and I growl. "You'll fit in here, I hope they don't move you."

"Listen *garçon*," he snorts at me, "I don't care how I was purchased but you guys need to get a refund, because as soon as I can, I'm getting all of us out."

"We don't hold anyone hostage." He growls, "you'll find many of the girls we help from those skin bags want to stay."

He shows me to a room and points to a shower. I groan at the sight, and he chuckles as he walks out the way we came in, the distinct sound of a bolt locking reaching my ears. We may be in fancier dwellings but we're still fucking prisoners. Not for long. I walk into the bathroom and when I see girly bath products, I squeal like a stuck pig. I strip out of my filthy clothes and start the shower.

I step out and feel like a brand-new woman, my skin smelling like papaya. I grab the terry robe from the back of the door and grab my belt from the floor, not caring about the rest. I head to the small closet and find a few white t-shirts with a few sweatshirt dress things. I get dressed in one of those and wrap my belt back around my waist, tying my long blonde hair up into a messy bun.

I find the communal kitchen and the girls are there stuffing their faces with more fruit. I sit down and decide to join in because I need the strength that comes with food and water.

"What is this place?" a girl asks. I didn't bother with names because I won't know them well beyond setting them free.

"A motorcycle club called Sharp Dentures." I shrug.

"Are they a bunch of old guys running the joint?" another asks.

"Don't care." I shrug. "I'm getting out so whoever wants to come is more than welcome."

"I wanna check it out first," one says and the rest murmur in agreement.

"Sure," I nod, finishing off my food.

I get up and walk over to the barn style door, laughing when I see it's made of wood. The lock I heard earlier was probably a slab of wood settling across, like you would find at a barn. I take my knife out of the holster and stab it through the slat, feeling it sink into the wooden slab. I begin to lift it straight up and once I feel it give away; I push the door open. It's now pitch-black outside but I can hear loud Metal music blaring from a large compound to my right. Some MC this is, no one felt the need to guard a bunch of females, and that's their fucking problem not mine.

I yank my knife back out and start for the building I saw them take Aniyah. If she's hurt any worse than when I last saw her, I will be blowing this place to fucking pieces. I open the door and find a young guy sitting on a chair in a leather vest.

"Hey!" he stands and I'm already across the room, slamming the butt end of my knife into his forehead. He slumps to the ground, and I roll my eyes. Too fucking easy.

It's one large room with curtains sectioning off areas and I stand in the center. Three of them are closed with the curtains. The first one has a guy with a nasty wound on his chest, the second one has another guy who's mumbling in his sleep, and the third is a female but not Aniyah. Looks like the party compound is getting a fucking surprise.

I stride back outside and start to walk across the compound when I hear tires squealing at the front gate.

Zander speeds along the dirt driveway, slamming down on the brakes and causing a cloud of dust to form around us. I'm not even thinking about the consequences of showing up at an MC club house unannounced, all I can focus on is the blonde bombshell in front of us.

She looks like a fucking deer caught in the headlights, as she fucking should.

Zander grabs Blaze's arm tightly before he can lunge at her, but I shove open my door and slam it behind me, not taking my eyes off her as I stalk towards her.

"Santos?" Selene squeaks out, all usual signs of bravery gone. She knows she fucked up by abandoning us, and I'm caught between wanting to kill her and fuck her. Or kill her while I fuck her, I'm not too sure yet.

"No, it's Father fucking Christmas," I grit out sarcastically. "You really thought you could outrun me? Outrun all fucking four of us?"

She looks ready to run in the opposite direction, smart girl, but she hesitates for too long, and my hand is wrapped around her slim throat and squeezing firmly before she can comprehend what's happening.

"You fucking left me!" I shout, squeezing harder until she squeaks out, "I'm sorry."

My grip loosens a fraction, just before I swoop down and claim her mouth with mine, my emotions running rampant inside me. I kiss her like she's the air I need to breathe, then I remember I'm pissed as fuck at her and fist her hair with my free hand, yanking her back to force her eyes up to mine.

"I could fucking kill you, Selene. Do you have any idea how fucked up we've been without you? How insane it drove me to not be with you while knowing you were putting yourself in danger like this?" I demand, her eyebrows shooting up in surprise.

"You knew where I was?" she pants quietly, appearing ready to knock me back and escape, but she doesn't. I snarl, towering over her, and I know I must look beyond murderous because she actually shrinks back the smallest amount.

"Of course we fucking did. Blaze has been following you since the moment you left. We will follow you to the depths of fucking Hell and back, baby. You should have known there'd be no escaping us."

I growl as she's pulled away from me, but I calm as Darius yanks her to his chest and kisses the living shit out of her, needing to feel her body against his to prove she's alright.

She smells fruity, and my dick swells as I think of all the ways I'm going to punish her for hurting me. She's lucky I don't shove granola bars up her ass and turn her into the world's prettiest vending machine.

"I'm going to fucking kill you," Darius murmurs against her lips, a breathy moan coming from her in response.

"You can try, asshole."

Zander and Blaze finally join us, and she turns her attention to the big angry bastard as he glares at her silently. "So, you were my stalker?"

He grunts, his lip lifting in a sneer. "You should have known it was me. I left you enough fucking hints. You know better than to keep your fucking windows unlocked too. Are you stupid?"

"Apparently," she says softly, her eyes flickering over him. "You really came for me?"

His sneer drops a fraction, but he holds his ground pretty well. "Of course, I did. You don't get to fuck me like you did and then bail. That's not how this shit works. Do you know how many opportunities I had to kill you? Your attention to detail is slacking," he barks, some of her cocky attitude returning as she snorts.

"Did you really have to leave a severed dick on my counter and your cum on my fucking coffee table? I assume that was your work of art, you fucking heathen."

He suddenly smirks darkly, stepping closer until he's looking down at her like she is his prey.

"I was getting pissed at watching you let those cunts touch you. What can I say? I was hoping you'd get the fucking hint and shut your fucking legs for five minutes," he answers, her eyes narrowing.

"It's none of your business what I do with my pussy, and I'm going to gut you for leaving your man spunk all over my fucking house," she seethes, but he grabs her by the throat and hauls her onto her tiptoes, getting in her face.

"Matter of fact, that pussy's ours, Selene. You never should have given us the deed to it if you never wanted it to be that way. Did you have fun fucking with us? Was it a way to kill time and get to Henry, was that it?"

"No! I just want to find my fucking sister!" she screams suddenly, anger pulsing through me. I manage to shove Blaze back, shrugging off Darius as he reaches for me.

"You didn't think we'd help you? I'd do anything for you, for fuck's sake! I'd have dropped everything at home to follow you, helping you day and night until we found her!" I spit, her eyes softening. Her emotions are fucking her up too, and I hope it fucking hurts.

"I couldn't drag you guys along. I needed..."

"Why the fuck not? What if something had gone wrong and you ended up dead? You might as well have aimed the gun at us and pulled the trigger yourself. We're nothing without you, baby. Fucking nothing," I force out.

She's suddenly kissing me, and I bite her lip sharply, a metallic tang spreading over my tongue as I dip it into her mouth. She moans, her fingernails digging into my back as she keeps me close, the demons in me wanting to be let out to punish her.

"Let's finish this at home," Zander grunts, snapping Selene out of our make-out session. She jerks back, pure rage written all over her face.

"I'm not going fucking anywhere, asshole. This is a lead and I need to stick it out. Besides, I need to help these women get out if these MC fuckers aren't good on their word," she spits, causing Zander's jaw to clench. We all want to get her ass home and punish her but dragging her away and wrecking her chance at finding her sister would cause us more grief than we'd like. We can punish her later.

Darius nods, dropping an arm around her shoulders to show he's on her side, the kiss ass.

"You think these guys are cool? You've spoken to them?" he asks, her body relaxing at his understanding tone.

"Yeah. They're apparently saving the women. It might be bullshit, but I want to make sure the women are safe before I leave. I have a friend here I want to find," she answers, making Blaze snort.

"The purple headed whore that tickles your clit?" he asks flatly, and Selene looks like she's seconds away from using his face as a punching bag.

"She's my friend and she was a mess when we were being transported here. The men are giving her medical help, apparently, so I want to make sure they fucking are. You're about to cop a fist to the face, grumpy," she hisses, but he simply glares back at her.

"Excellent. Because you're about to cop my fist right up your cunt."

Zander rolls his eyes at their banter, while Darius and I grin with amusement. I wish I could be there the next time Blaze gets her hot little body under him, because I bet, they'll put on a fucking show.

"Are we checking shit out, or what? I'm bored," I declare, moving towards the sound of the music. I do love a good party.

Selene chases after Santos, bitching him out about just wandering into an MC's hangout, leaving us to trail behind them. Blaze takes up the rear, keeping his eyes peeled as Zander and I talk.

"Do you think these guys are legit?" I ask, hearing him scoff.

"Legit? No. They might be trying to help women, but I doubt there's not a catch. Is she seriously about to just walk right through the door?" he growls, a smirk tugging at my lips as she grabs the door handle and flings it open, snarking at Santos as he walks so close to her that he almost knocks her over. He isn't going to let her out of his sight ever again, I hope she knows that.

People are glancing our way, but Selene stalks right over to one of them and starts talking, her hands moving around with angry motions. I assume the dude's going to haul her ass back to the other women, but a booming laugh leaves him as he grins.

His eyes move up to us as we approach, and he raises an eyebrow in question. "You think wandering in here is a smart move, my friend?"

"My girl's worth the bullets. I ain't *your* shit," Zander growls, his fingers twitching, ready for a fight. The guy chuckles, eyeing Blaze for a moment before motioning to Selene.

"She mentioned you four to my boy when she got here. I'm Coin." He offers his hand and I give it a dirty look, but Zander steps forward, moving into the leader roll that he seems to end up with.

"Zander. This is Darius, Santos, and the guy behind me is Blaze. You like buying skin?" he asks bluntly, Coin giving him an amused smile.

"We'd prefer the term, freeing. The girls we end up with are usually in terrible condition, so we feed them, hydrate them, and get them back on their feet."

"Then you fucking keep them by the look of things," Santos snaps, his sharp eyes moving around the room at the few women. Coin laughs, leaning back on his heels to cross his arms.

"None of them are here by force. A lot choose to stick around, others leave once they're healthy enough. May I ask why the fuck you're all here? I'm surprised you didn't take off, blondie," he states as he turns his attention to Selene, her lips lifting in a sneer.

"My friend. Where is she?"

"She's being treated. You can see her tomorrow when she's rested. You don't seem like a girl who'd allow herself to be snatched and sold," he observes, her eyebrow lifting a fraction.

"I was investigating the missing women. I'm looking for answers about my sister who went missing when I was a teenager. I have a hunch that you fuckers might know something about that."

He shrugs, looking thoughtful for a moment before replying. "Your best bet at finding out information on any of the girls we've been in contact with, would be Papi Loco. He's not here right now though, so stick around and grab a beer or something. No threatening my brothers, alright? I'm looking at you, shifty eyes," he grins, cocking his head at Santos who puffs out his chest.

"I only bring out my weapons if I need to," he exclaims, making me snort.

"No, you don't."

He flips me the bird, turning his attention to Selene as Coin walks off, trusting us to behave for some stupid reason. His casual approach to us is grating on my nerves a little.

Zander and Blaze grumble something about checking the bar out, giving me a look to tell me we better be good. Fat chance.

Santos backs Selene up until her ass is pressed against my front, my hands dropping instantly to her waist. He leans down, his voice low and full of promise.

"You're in so much trouble, babe. You won't be able to sit down once we're through with you."

She shivers, trying to stand her ground but failing, her body responding to his voice by pressing back into me further.

"Do your worst, fuckface."

There are people everywhere, but a dark corner isn't hard to find, and I tug her back as Santos follows, his eyes burning into her with the threat of violence. The moment my back hits the wall, my teeth and lips are on her neck, sucking and biting my way across her skin and breathing her in.

Santos doesn't give a shit if anyone sees us or not as he shoves his hand up her skirt, not wasting time as he pushes his fingers inside her roughly. She moans loudly, the music drowning it out as he pumps his arm at a punishing pace.

Every time he gets her close, he pulls back, starting all over again until she's growling.

"Let me come, you piece of shit," she snaps, a crazy laugh spilling from his lips as he hauls her forward, tugging her further into the room. The lighting isn't the best, lucky for her, otherwise everyone in the entire room will be seeing her getting nailed in a second. I see him fiddle with the front of his sweatpants and grin.

"You don't fucking deserve to," he bites out, hiking her thigh up around his waist, appearing to be dirty dancing against her, but I know differently from the way Selene's body reacts. She gasps, her back arching into me as a low chuckle vibrates from my chest.

"Did you miss us, baby? Did you think about us when you had someone else's dick inside you?" I ask roughly. She curses, nodding her head as Santos grinds his dick into her pussy, her butt pressing back against my groin.

I slip a hand up her skirt and pull her panties aside, running my fingers through her juices and along Santos' length as it moves in and out of her, gathering the wetness to slide it up her crack. She gasps as I press a finger against her tight hole, easing it inside her slowly while sinking my teeth into her shoulder.

"All we've done since you left is think about all the ways we could fucking punish you for leaving us. Do you understand why we're pissed?" I growl, biting her sharply again when she doesn't answer.

"I should have told you guys, I get it," she snarls, but she grinds her body between us, telling us she's not even mad.

I add a second finger, stretching her more as I unzip my jeans and pull my dick free, sliding it between her legs. Santos pulls out, pulling her forwards to kiss, while not hesitating to reach between her legs for my dick, helping to guide it into her dripping pussy.

She moans into his mouth, her walls clamping around me as I grind into her, wanting to get my dick as wet as possible. I wanted to punish her, but I didn't particularly want to tear her ass up in the literal sense.

The people and sounds around us fade as I finally slide into her ass, a groan leaving me as Santos pushes inside her pussy again. We grind into her, building her up just to withhold her release.

"Please," she grits out, but we ignore her and chase our own releases, not giving into her pleading. I come first, biting into her neck so hard I draw blood, and the second I pull out of her and fix my pants, Santos backs her into the wall again and fucks her hard, not giving a shit if he gets caught.

Selene starts cursing, her body tense as it gets ready to explode, but Santos slams in hard, filling her pussy with his cum and pulling out, fisting her hair to make her focus on him.

"A few weeks of fucking you without letting you finish is looking mighty appealing, babe. Stay with Darius, I need a drink." Then he releases his hold on her and fixes his pants, stalking off in the direction of the bar without another word.

Selene's fuming, her fists balling at her sides as she glares at his retreating back. I lean against the wall, running my eyes over her as if to make sure she really is here.

"You hurt us. You fucking broke Santos," I say, her eyes swinging my way as if she forgot I'm here. She goes to swing at me, but I catch her wrist firmly, tugging her closer. "You fucking broke him, Selene. I was by his side every second of the fucking day, getting my ass beat so he could let out some of his demons instead of going after you and massacring everyone in the process. He's been blind drunk, he's cried, he's screamed until his lungs gave out, and I took the brunt of his emotions because I'd do anything to stop his hurting. I'd do the same for you, so why the fuck didn't you just ask us to come with you? I thought we were a team?" I ask, confusion flickering in her pretty eyes.

"I'm not your problem. I'm not worth your life, D," she replies softly, only just loud enough for me to hear over the racket around us. I snort, releasing her and shaking my head.

"You're not a problem, baby. You're a part of us, and it's about time you realize just how much you mean to us. You're not a possession. You're not a mountain we conquered. You're a part of our fucking family, and you ripped us apart when you left. If Santos is only withholding orgasms from you for a while, you got off lightly in my eyes," I state, stepping forward to grip her chin gently. "You're not a lone wolf anymore. Fucking face that fact so we can all move on and find your fucking sister together."

She wants to argue, I can see it on her face, but she finally wraps her arms around my waist and presses her cheek to my chest, surprising me slightly.

"I missed you too," is all she says, but it's as close to an apology as I'll get, so I put my arms around her and hold her tightly, simply happy to have her back.

Reaped

Chapter Sixteen

Zander

"I think they're fucking each other." I state as I slug back half the fucking beer in my hand.

"And she fucking called *me* a heathen." Blaze grumbles over his neat scotch. For a nasty looking brute he sure likes a fancy man's drink.

"How much do you want to bet they fill both her holes with cum and leave her hanging?"

Finally, a small smirk settles over his lips, yanking on the white skin of his scar, "how about we join in on that?"

He's never one to play around like this and I can feel something settle in my chest with his admission, Blaze has fallen just as hard for her as the rest of us. I never thought I would see the day that he let himself give in to anyone outside of the four of us. His upbringing ensured that he would never trust anyone wholly and the things he endured sealed his heart in cement, until her. Luckily, we all feel the same way and us sharing her keeps us together.

"I'm down." I nod, gulping down the rest of my beer.

We turn and watch as Selene separates herself from Darius and walks towards a group of girls. They smile at her, but I can see the wariness in their eyes. They point her down a hallway and I snort.

"Bet she has a lot of cleaning up to do. Think of how much build up we have." I grin at Blaze.

"I can't wait to fill it right the fuck back up. You take her pussy; I'm shoving my cock in her ass." He growls, throwing back his drink.

I cringe at the thought of Blaze's dick forcing its way into her tight asshole, I hope she has life insurance. Another beer is placed in front of me and another drink in front of Blaze. Santos appears, squeezing between us, and looks completely sated.

"How was it?" I ask and he shoots me a grin.

"Like sticking my dick in a fruit cup, wet and sweet."

"What the fuck?" Blaze growls.

"She smells like fruit." Santos shrugs, "and she was fucking dripping wet."

"Did she come?"

Santos laughs maniacally and shakes his head, "not gonna happen. You lot better not let her either, we need to band together for this."

Blaze and I nod, a ghost of a smile on his scary face. "Did you find out anything about this place when your dick wasn't stuck in a fruit cup?" Blaze growls.

"Let's call her pussy a fruit cup forever." Santos snaps his fingers. "And yes," he nods, "I was speaking to the bartender - his name is Licker - get it? Like liquor but it's L-I-C-K-E-R."

"Yes," I roll my eyes, "go on."

"Clever fuckers here," he chuckles, "anyway, they call themselves Dientes Afilado - that means Sharp Teeth - and they've been around for a long time. They may not like to sell skin, but they sell just about everything else. Drugs and weapons being their most profitable."

"Licker told you all this in one sitting?" I raise my brow.

"I think Licker had his tongue in some liquor." He shrugs and I groan at his stupid joke, "so the Pres. is a guy named Papi Loco and he's an old son of a bitch. As mean as a bull, he likes killing, and he likes to leave body parts as gifts to people who wrong him. His Vice Pres. is named Loquito and is also his son. Just as crazy and unhinged. But really, they sound like my kind of people. Licker warned me that they are batshit but love their people."

"Sounds like you'd fit in here." Blaze grunts.

"Don't worry, you sexy ass fucker," Santos bats his eyelashes at him, "I will never leave you. I only recognize one Papi around here."

I choke on my beer as Santos blows him a fucking kiss and walks back over to Darius.

"Some days I swear that fucker is suicidal." Blaze says, unperturbed by Santos' antics.

"I hope us being here doesn't set Papi fuckface off, I'm not prepared for a shootout. I couldn't bring my machine gun on the flight."

Blaze gives me a little snort and I relax seeing him finally let that dark part of him recede. I saw the moment he released it. He was ripping John's ribs apart and now I want to gag again, just thinking of it.

"Looks like she cleared the dumpster," Blaze snarks and I look over to find Selene exiting a corridor.

"Too bad for her, today is garbage day." I retort.

"My cum ain't garbage." Blaze sneers.

"It is if you're calling her pussy a dumpster."

"Touché." He nods and downs his drink, "let's give our Little Reaper a scare."

"Does she have her knife on her?" I give her a once over.

"Yep," Blaze nods, "she thinks that belt hides it."

I stare at the belt, trying to see the knife, and Blaze flicks my ear, "you're as dumb as nails, you know that?"

"Fuck you, I hope she stabs you first." I stalk towards Selene.

The moment she sees me, her eyes widen, and then widen further when she sees Blaze behind me.

"No," she shakes her head, "not you two. I will kill someone tonight if you try that same shit."

I grab her by the throat and yank her into me, pressing my mouth to hers. "You don't get a fucking say any longer, Reaper. You take whatever the fuck we give you and you smile while it's happening." I flick my tongue against her bottom lip, and she snaps at it, making me laugh.

"Are you gonna dance with me, grumpy?" she asks Blaze over my shoulder, not the slightest bit worried about my hand around her throat.

"The only dancing you'll be doing is over this cock." He retorts.

"I remember our last dance," she moans and licks her lips, "I can't wait for an encore."

My cock swells painfully and I need to rip it out of my pants, then sink it into her. I've never gone this long without sex and that gives me another reason to be pissed off at her. How dare she give me something I will never be able to find anywhere else? I turn us around and shove her back into Blaze's chest, my hand still wrapped around her throat. The bitch doesn't flinch, if anything she looks like she's ready to combust, and I can't let that happen. I made my boy a promise.

I lean over her shoulder and whisper in Blaze's ear, "avoid the clit."

He gives me a brusque nod as I lean back down and look at Selene, her eyes hooded.

"Are you two going to kiss?" Her voice is breathy.

"Wrong duo," I growl, "but don't worry, we'll soon remind you who we are."

"So, show me," she says as she yanks her skirt up around her waist.

I sandwich her tight between us and look around the room, expecting other men to have their eyes on my woman. But all I see are naked girls, some dancing and others fucking, just like we're planning to do. I fucking like it here.

I step back and undo my belt, my cock straining to be set free. Blaze reaches down and rips her thong clear off her body, holding it up to his nose. "Smells like cum."

"I was filled like an eclair," she makes a grab for the scrap of fabric, "what the fuck do you expect?"

"I've always been partial to the Boston Cream," I say as I hitch her leg over my hip and begin to rub my cock through her already soaking pussy.

"Yes, Zander. Fuck, Boston Cream me." She begins to shake, her body begging for a release, and I pull away.

"Did you think I was going first?"

"What?" She looks up at me with lust and confusion.

My cock is out in my hand and the metal through the tip glints. I reach between her legs and grab her arousal, feeling her shudder between Zan and I. I grab an ass cheek and spread her wide, lining myself up. I feel her tense as soon as my head touches her puckered hole, and she begins to shake her head.

"No Blaze," she begs, and I grow even harder, "you won't fit."

"Let's find out," I lean into her ear while pushing against her tight hole. "Take a deep breath."

"No," she continues to shake her head, but her pleas fall on deaf ears. I won't be taking any mercy on her, or her dumpster.

My head breaches her ass but it's so fucking tight, and I do fear I'm going to cause some damage. She's whining as her head falls back on my chest, her own chest heaving, and sweat forming on her temples.

"Does it hurt?" Zander asks as he reaches between them and slowly begins to push into her.

"Yes," she moans, "so fucking good."

I grab the back of her head and shove her forward into Zander, the impact of her forehead to his chest jarring them both. Zander bottoms out inside of her but his chest rumbles with laughter as I use this new angle to plummet my length all the way in. She screams into his chest, and I'm not bothered if it's in pleasure or pain at this point. I yank her head back up and begin thrusting in time with Zander, our cocks rubbing together through the thin layer separating us.

She reaches down to rub her clit, but Zander grabs her hand up and winds it around his head, he chuckles at what I imagine to be a scowl on our Reaper's face. I look down to watch myself disappear inside her, grinning when I see some blood; knowing her scream was one of pain. I continue plowing into her, Zander doing the same from the front, and when I feel her tighten, we both still.

"No," she growls, grabbing Zander's chin. "Do not fucking think about it."

As soon as she's relaxed again and she lets out a groan, I slam it back home. I chase my release and it feels so fucking good to finally be inside of her again. I can see Zander doing the same and we both thrust one final time, spilling ourselves into her. I feel her clench around us, trying to work herself over, and grinding into us. But it's no use when we both abruptly pull out and I spread her open to watch my cum mixed with her blood seep out.

She yanks her skirt down and shoves Zander out of the way, stalking off back to the bathroom. We're both tucking ourselves in when I hear a whistle behind me. I turn and find two bikers, mean as fuck looking. They're staring us down and I don't break eye contact as I shove my cock back in my pants.

"That's your woman?" One of them juts his chin towards Selene.

"Something like that," I grunt at the same time Zander says "yes."

"What are you guys doing here?" he asks, and we walk over to them.

"Chasing down skin sellers and trying to locate her sister that went missing a long time ago." I answer him.

"Skin sellers huh? We're doing the same thing. We have an axe to grind too." I take a good look at them and begin to see the resemblance.

"Kho." The one talking nods at us, "this is my twin brother, Khaine."

Zander snorts beside me and I look back and forth between them, "are you for real? Your names are cocaine?"

"Kho and Khaine." Khaine shrugs and grins. "It is now anyways."

"What's with the names in this place?" Zander chuckles.

"Pres. lives up to his name, but he's given us all a chance to start over and shed who we were before." Kho explains. "We were picked up by a skin seller when we were fourteen and Papi L saved us. Now we're in charge of distribution."

"Of cocaine." I take a wild fucking guess.

"Yes!" They exclaim together.

"I feel like we're in Wonderland." I tell Zander and laughter rips from his mouth.

"I fucking love it here." He says as tears build up in his eyes with the force of his laugh.

I feel a sharp slap on my ass and turn, my fist lifted. Selene stands there with her brow raised, taunting me, and grinning when I lower it.

"You made my ass bleed you fucking animal." She yells and I snort.

I wrap my arm around her shoulder and haul her in beside me, "I'm gonna do it again later."

The guys in front of us are smiling and laughing as Selene looks between them, "who the fuck are you?"

She always sounds like she owns wherever the fuck she's standing, lacking any respect for the people who actually own it, and I can't help that my cock swells with pride.

"This is Kho and Khaine." Zander says, his voice still holding a bit of humor.

"Great," she nods, "can you guys make the pain in my ass disappear?"

They both grab their stomachs and laugh, finding the Little Reaper under my arm amusing. Little do they know, she'd have no problem bleeding them out here, and in front of an audience. And I'm rock fucking solid again.

"Do either of you know a girl named Jan? Or Janelle?" she asks, and they both crinkle their brows in thought.

"No," they shake their heads together, looking very much like Tweedle Dee and Dum. "Who is she?"

"My sister," Selene's shoulders slump. "She was taken and sold when I was younger."

The one named Khaine stares into her face, studying her features, and when I growl, he gives me a lazy grin. "Boss tries to keep track of who's passed through here, so you can talk to him when he's back."

"When will that be?" Selene huffs.

"Tomorrow morning." Kho nods, "I'll have Sunshine make up a room for you. I'm assuming one is good?"

"Yes," Zander says when I say, "no."

"C'mon," Selene coos, "we'll play hide the pickles."

I roll my eyes at her remark as everyone else laughs.

"Sunshine!" Khaine calls out and an older lady with a scowl that could rival my own comes over. Sunshine my fucking ass. "Can you set these guys up with a room for the night?"

Sunshine has frizzy, bleached hair that stands up in all directions, the damaged strands no longer smooth. Her face is wrinkled, and she has deep creases around her mouth from smoking too fucking much. Her saggy tits are forced into a push-up bra, and they rival her face for wrinkles. I shudder when I'm done with my once over.

"Who the fuck are they?" her voice sounds like she smokes a pack of cigarettes a day, "how do we know they won't gut us in the middle of the night?"

"Because I just got double dicked down, twice." Selene growls at her, "I'm fucking tired. The only blood spilling will belong to my men for not letting me come."

Her men. I hate that I love the sound of that so much. The two women stare each other down and Santos comes up to us with Darius in tow.

"Kho and Khaine!" Santos exclaims and I roll my eyes, of course he's met them.

"San!" They exclaim right back, bumping his fist with their own.

When Selene tosses him a questioning glare, Santos shrugs, "I met them earlier when I was grabbing a drink. Licker introduced us."

Sunshine grumbles a bit more but motions for us to follow her. She takes us down the corridor that Selene disappeared in for the bathroom and then up a set of stairs. The second floor is a labyrinth of interconnecting corridors, all of them lined with doors.

"This one is a guest room." She says as she opens the door. Inside is a king size bed, thankfully, and a couch as well. Then she shuts it behind us, leaving quickly.

"A ray of sunshine indeed." Zander remarks.

"Do you think we'll get names here?" Santos' eyes light up.

"Yeah," I grunt, "you two will be Don and Key." I swing my finger between him and Darius.

They both hoot and start laughing, "was that a joke, Daddy?" Santos exclaims and I storm away from them into the adjoining bathroom. I refuse to engage.

When I finish up and step back out, it's like a fucking preschool classroom. Everyone is bickering.

"One of you is getting between my legs and licking me clean. I refuse to sleep without coming." Selene stomps her foot.

"Should've thought of that before you ran off." Zander growls.

"Fine!" She crawls up the bed, her ass and pussy on full display under her skirt. "I'll do it myself." She reaches between her legs as we all stand in a line at the foot of the bed, watching as she begins to play with her clit.

Just as she really begins to pant and her pussy is glistening with arousal, Darius jumps on the bed. He grabs both her hands as Santos holds her feet, wrapping a belt around her two wrists and straps her to the bedpost.

"Not tonight, Reaper." Santos says, kissing her foot as she kicks it out.

"Undo this right now." She struggles against the bonds.

Zan, Santos, and Darius climb up on the bed, ignoring her demands as I fall onto the couch.

"Fuck, I'm beat." I groan and everyone chuckles. All save for the Little Reaper who is doling out death threats.

REAPED

Chapter Seventeen

Santos

The click of a gun has my eyes springing open, the sun peeking through the crack in the curtains and reflecting off the weapon in question. I squint, my tired eyes adjusting and zoning in on the man standing beside the bed.

I don't even hesitate before throwing myself out of bed and slamming my shoulder into the guy, landing on top of him as we hit the ground. The commotion wakes the others up, but I don't look their way as I wrestle the gun from the prick and crack my elbow against his jaw, his head snapping to the side with a psychotic laugh.

"You're a fucking wild one!" he cackles before throwing his weight up and managing to buck me off, scrambling to his knees and pulling another gun from nowhere. He aims it at my face, a cocky smirk stretching across his lips. "What now, asshole?"

I grin, confusing him a fraction. "I'm not the real threat in the room."

One of the guys must have untied Selene while we were rolling around on the fucking floor, because she moves up behind him silently and wraps one of the belts tightly around his neck to yank him back sharply, a choked sound leaving the guy in surprise.

My girl has balls of steel, because she stands over him and shoves a foot down on his chest hard the moment he lands on his back, glaring down the barrel of his gun without flinching.

"You think you can touch one of my guys and live to fucking tell the tale?" she snaps, her eyes filling with heat. Hell fucking no. I get to my feet and stand beside her, growling at him like an animal.

He quirks an eyebrow at me before turning his attention back to Selene, his voice amused. "It's been a while since a woman got that rough with me. You want to play, kitty cat?"

I snarl and lift my gun to shoot his stupid face, but Selene elbows me in the ribs hard, causing me to drop the gun into her waiting hand.

"The deal was we wouldn't fucking threaten any of Coin's brothers, dumbass," she says swiftly, narrowing her eyes when I wave my hands in the asshole's direction.

"Excuse the fuck out of me then, because when someone's pointing their gun in my face, I don't usually stick to a moral code of respect. I also never agreed to his request," I spit, relaxing as Darius moves in beside me and rests his hand on my hip, squeezing firmly to draw my attention off the smug bastard on the ground at our girl's feet.

He laughs, the sound loud in the small room.

"You're friends with Coin? Why didn't you fucking say so! His brothers are my brothers! Or *piñatas*, depending on the situation. Right now, you could be either, so you want to tell me who the fuck you are and why the fuck you're sleeping in my club house?"

"Not particularly," Selene deadpans, not removing her foot from him. "How about you tell us who the fuck you are?"

"I guess I'll play your little game since you asked so nicely, *Mamacita*," he winks.

Selene's foot moves up towards his throat pressing down. "I'm not a little mama, asshole."

"Give me twenty minutes of your time and you will be," he wheezes as she applies more pressure, and lucky for him, Darius grabs my arm to yank me back before I can beat the shit out of him.

Zander's standing close to me too, so I know they're hoping I don't get us all shot at. They'll want to beat the prick too, so they can fuck off if they don't think I'm going to kill him.

"Name!" Selene snaps, sick of his bullshit like we are.

He rolls his eyes and waits until she removes her foot a little before speaking.

"I'm Loquito."

"I could have told you that," I growl, but he ignores me and keeps his eyes on Selene as she assesses the situation. She finally steps back, allowing him to get to his feet.

"You're the VP?" she asks, her eyes lighting up with hope. "Is Papi Loco back too?"

His eyes narrow at her questions, but Zander steps forward and offers his hand like the good boy he is, so I step back to sit on the bed, grabbing my jeans off the floor.

"I'm Zander. Coin told us to stick around because Papi Loco might be able to help us with a problem."

Loquito doesn't look convinced, but he holds a hand out to shake.

"What kind of problem?"

"A missing woman problem," Selene states firmly, giving me a dirty look as she watches me quietly pull my knife from the pocket of my jeans. "Hey, *estúpido*. Stand down unless directed otherwise."

I grumble as I step into my pants, shoving the knife into my pocket again. "You're no fun."

"Oh, I'm sorry. Am I not giving out a happy vibe this morning?" she hisses, causing my dick to twitch behind my zipper.

"Baby, you're giving my dick a happy vibe. Tone down the flirting, we have company," I grin, chuckling as she flips me the bird. Loquito is watching us closely, his eyes darting back to me every so often. He doesn't like me? Well, good, because I don't like him either.

I roll my eyes as Zander starts spilling his guts about why we're here, Selene glaring at me regularly as I keep giving Loquito dirty looks. The moment he turns his back, I'm going to put a bullet in him.

As if knowing my evil plans, Darius sits on the bed and hauls me back, dropping an arm over my middle to get comfortable.

"What's up with you?" he whispers, my eyes dropping to him as he sinks his teeth into my bare peck, pulling a growl from me.

"I don't like being woken up with a gun in my face. Sue me for being sensitive about the matter."

"You are being a little extra for someone who got laid last night," he teases, and I can't fight the grin as it spreads across my face.

"I'd hate to know how pissy she's going to be today. I might fuck her again after lunch and not let her get off," I murmur, Darius is hooting with laughter and drawing attention to us. Blaze is sitting on the couch with a gun in his hand, playing guard dog as usual, but Zander, Selene, and Loquito all glance over at us with a frown.

I laugh too, only making Selene's annoyance stronger. "What the fuck is so funny?"

"Nothing, babe. Go back to your conversation," Darius chuckles, but she stomps over and smacks me in the back of the head.

"Hey! What was that for?!" I bark, but she leans in close so that her breath fans over my lips.

"You know exactly what that's for, you bastard," she growls, her fist landing against my ribs as I grab her waist and haul her on top of me. I bite her neck sharply, but before I can taunt her some more, Zander snatches her arm and tugs her away from me.

"For fuck's sake. Fuck around later, you two. We have shit to deal with. Loquito was about to show us where to go for breakfast."

Loquito barks out a laugh, his eyes bright and alert as if he's just shoved his face into a bag of cocaine and inhaled the hell out of it.

"Was I now?"

"Yes. You need to tell us about where Papi Loco is," Selene retorts, looking back at me with a scowl. "I'm sure you two can get along over breakfast. You guys are so similar it's scary."

I snort, glaring at Loquito as I get to my feet, snatching my shirt up and pulling it over my head.

"I'm not sitting near this cunt. Not even for you."

I eye Santos as we all sit at the table, one of the women scurrying around and bringing us plates of food. Loquito keeps smirking at him, causing anger to pulse through him in waves, and I won't be surprised if he snaps and lunges over the table at him.

Selene's usual moaning draws my attention as she licks bacon grease from her fingers, Blaze and Zander staring at her like hawks. I don't blame them; our girl makes food feel like a sexual experience.

"So, you want to speak to my dad?" Loquito finally asks, Selene snapping her head his way.

"Yes. Coin claims he'd be the man to speak with," she confirms, surprisingly forgetting about her food as she continues to watch him. You know she's seriously in thought when the food stops being shoveled into her mouth as if she were a Hungry Hippo game. My girl's far from a hippo, but you know what I mean.

"This girl must be important. Where are you guys from?" he questions. "I haven't seen you around, and I think I'd remember you."

Santos' fork bends in his grip, and Blaze snatches it from beside him, slamming it down on the table.

"Act civilized for once in your fucking life, you crazy prick."

Santos' lip lifts in a sneer, but Loquito grins.

"He's fine, we're all a little crazy around here. Besides, I'd stab myself too if I were him. I'm assuming the sexy lady at the table is his woman?" he taunts, and I dig my fingers into Santos' thigh to give him something to focus on. Thankfully, they ignore his jab.

He growls under his breath, but he grabs a buttered roll from the table and shoves it into his mouth like a savage, chewing loudly and earning a dark glare from Blaze.

"Anyway. Tell me about the chick you're looking for. Who is she?" Loquito continues as if Santos isn't about to murder him with the butter knife he's currently eyeing while he chews.

"She's my sister. She was taken a long time ago. I assumed she was dead, but the more I looked, the more I discovered hints that she wasn't. I've basically spent my entire life searching for her," Selene says firmly, but I hear the emotion in her tone that she's trying to hide.

Zander drops an arm over her shoulders, appearing casual, but we know it's to give her comfort discreetly. Loquito's eyes dart over to Santos, seeming surprised that he isn't flipping out. When he doesn't rip his shirt off and Hulk smash the table, Loquito slides his eyes back to Selene and cocks his head.

"And you think Papi Loco had something to do with that?"

I can see her eyes blazing with annoyance, and I know she doesn't trust these MC cunts at all, so I quickly speak to stop the argument before it starts.

"No. We think maybe she's come through in one of the shipments you've helped save. Why do you save them, anyway?" I quiz, his eyes narrowing to slits.

"Why the fuck wouldn't we? We're crazy, not heartless. No woman should be taken and sold like cattle. Most of those women end up beaten and raped until their bodies give out."

"So, you guys don't have strip clubs and hookers?" Santos snaps.

"We do, but they're all employed the old-fashioned way. All the women that get on their back or knees are here because they choose to be, no one's forcing their hand. That's not how we roll," he snorts, looking back at Selene with a softer expression. "If your sister came through here, Dad would know for sure."

"So, where the fuck is he?" Selene grumbles, causing a breath of annoyance to leave Blaze. Loquito isn't bothered though, and he snatches a buttery roll and takes a bite, grinning at Santos to agitate him some more.

"I left earlier than him. He'll be here soon though, don't stress. If any of you guys need some company, the girls…"

A knife whizzes past his head, slamming into the wall behind him, and he raises an eyebrow at Selene who's fuming. "Oh, it's like that is it, *Tormenta Pequeña*?" he teases, but his eyes turn serious as Blaze growls a warning.

When Zander's arm tightens around Selene a little more, Loquito nods.

"Respect. Apologies, I didn't realize you were all spoken for."

"I'm still not sorry for throwing the knife," Selene grunts and shovels bacon into her mouth as if she never stopped.

His eyes light up with amusement, a chuckle leaving him as he leans back in his chair.

"I'd be disappointed if you were."

Selene's right. It's scary how alike this dude is to Santos. From the way he holds himself and speaks, right down to some of his looks. Those crazy eyes? Mirror image of my boy's.

Selene

There's something about Loquito that doesn't sit right with me, the fucker is shifty, and he makes me want to see how many holes I can poke into him within a minute. I suck the bacon grease off my fingers and moan at the salty goodness, my pussy throbs, threatening to combust over pig meat. So fucking good though.

Blaze clears his throat and I roll my eyes knowing it's directed at me without even looking at the fucker.

"I don't like your shifty eyes," I point at Loquito, and he laughs heartily, "and you're clearly a few screws short of a box."

He keeps the smile firmly on his face as he leans on the table, "it's one thing to talk to me like that, I really don't give a shit about how people see me, but do not think you can speak to my father like that. And another word of advice? Don't speak to Henny."

"Henny?"

"That's my pop's old lady." Loquito nods as he scratches his head with the barrel of his gun.

"Why can't we speak to some old woman?" Santos snarls, "we have the best pussy around, we don't want an old one."

"She ain't old, man," Loquito laughs, "that's just what we call our women. She's young but she's feisty and she won't think twice about clawing your eyes out."

"Whatever," I shrug, "I'm not here for Hen or whoever."

"You're trained, Loqi has the eye." He taps the gun off his temple.

"Loqi?" I snort, "yes I'm trained."

"But why?" he stares at me with real curiosity, "why did you become the Reaper Incarnate?"

The tables fall into an immediate hush, and I see Santos tense in my peripheral.

"Sorry, what?" I crinkle my nose in confusion.

He leans back and chuckles, looking relaxed despite the large men around the table looking ready to pounce on him, "Henry Walton used to provide us with some girls, boys, anything really, and then we heard he was carved up like a Christmas ham. A Reaper's mark left on his body like so many of his associates before him. Not that we'd miss the fuck. Then Mack Delaney let us know he could pull up the slack with this new guy John down here in Nevada. So, we agreed, hunting down skin trades in our own state is easier, and we were up for the challenge."

"Only you didn't succeed," Santos snarks.

"Nope, someone got to John before us, made a real mess too, but no reaper mark on his body. Not like the other bodies found around Vegas."

John is dead? I look at each one of my guys and realize that would've been the only way they found me. I'm fucking pissed that I can't live up to the promise I made to Dempster, but I'm glad it led them to me.

The table stays quiet, and I curse myself for being such a fucking celebrity. It's hard being famous. "Not *all* of the Vegas ones were me." I say and he hoots again as I give Blaze a dark look. I still can't believe the asshole posed as the Reaper Incarnate, the fucking nerve.

"You still haven't answered my question." He leans in again and I see the sharp intelligence in his eyes.

"I know," I lean in as well, "I don't need to explain myself to anyone, *Loqi.*"

"Perc and Vico have a theory," he grins. "They think you were raised by skin traders, being prostituted out and then you snapped. But I just saw your Reaper tattoo this morning and pieced it together."

"Perc and Vico?" Zander snorts. "Pill pushers?"

"Fucking Wonderland." Blaze retorts.

"I raised myself." I shrug and leave it at that.

"I love a mystery." He winks at me.

"Loqi!" We all turn and see Kho and Khaine striding into the dining hall. "Papi is twenty minutes out."

Loqi gets up from the table and taps his knuckles on the wooden top, "I'll let him know that you want to speak to him."

I give him a nod and then watch as he walks out of the room with a slow steady swagger, the walk so fucking familiar to me.

"That guy is a fucking noodle dick." Santos snarls and I turn to look at him.

"Noodle dick?" I grin, "how do you know that? You feel it while you were tussling?"

"Nope," he smirks right back at me, the sexy fucker, "I didn't feel a damn thing, that's why, noodle dick."

Darius snorts as he's drinking and begins to choke as Zander pats his back.

"Bunch of fucking clowns." Blaze mutters but I can see the slight ghost of a smile on his face.

I don't know why I ever thought leaving them was a good idea, they were made for me, and each in their own way. I finally found a family after Jan, and I almost destroyed it with my denial. I thought I would never find anyone on the same frequency as me and instead I found four. It will take nothing short of an apocalypse to separate us now.

Chapter Eighteen

Selene

I'm wound so fucking tight and I know if I could just get off, I would feel so much better. I could do it myself but it's the damn principle, I have four guys with big ass dicks that should be doing it for me. On top of that, I'm punishing myself just as much as they are, I shouldn't have run from them. I can't keep blaming shit on my mommy issues or the fact that my life wasn't rainbows and roses, I should've trusted them.

I'm lying on the bed in the room we're staying in, waiting for my large breakfast to digest, and trying to forget about the pulsing in my cunt.

"A lot can be accomplished in twenty minutes." Darius murmurs as he starts to crawl up my body.

I jam my knee up and into his balls, twisting to watch him howl in pain. "I'm not in the mood for more of your games." I sit up, "I've gathered a liking for pussy recently, maybe I can find a suitable replacement for four limp dicks."

"Watch it, Reaper." Blaze growls from his perch on the couch, "nothing about me is limp. I'll make you swallow those words."

Santos is standing over Darius, rubbing his buzzed head but smirking as he continues to moan, "so, you want some clubhouse whore? Their pussies are used like a merry go round."

"I wonder what they name their club whores." Zander snickers.

"I would name mine *Puss in Boots*." I say proudly and all the guys laugh, including Blaze.

I give them all a dirty look and head to the door, "maybe it'll be a set of twins, Puss and Boots."

They all laugh riotously behind me, and I grab the handle in my hand. Just as I'm about to turn it, I feel a warm body at my back.

"Take your hand off the door, Reaper." Blaze's hand grabs my hair and yanks my head back, "or don't, either way, I'm ready to fucking punish you."

"About time, asshole." I growl just before his mouth lands on mine in a punishing kiss.

He drags us both backward towards the bed just as Zander hits my front and begins to lift my shirt. "Naughty, Reaper." He mutters just as his mouth latches around my nipple. The sensation shoots straight down to my sopping wet pussy, making it clench with need.

"If one of you doesn't make me come, I'm stabbing every fucker in this fucking compound." I snarl and Blaze chuckles as his mouth moves down my neck.

Blaze moves from behind me and shoves me down on the bed, my back bouncing off the plush mattress. I look up and find Darius standing over my head, his cock in his hand. He wears a sly smirk, and I can't help the one I give in response.

"Kiss and make it better." He says as he drags me toward him, making my head hang off the side.

I open my mouth wide and laugh when he hesitates, "come on, let Mama kiss your boo-boo."

Darius' eyes roll back into his head as I take him into my mouth. My head at the perfect angle for him to fuck my throat. I feel my pants being pulled off my legs and when I feel the brutality of the mouth between them, I know it's Blaze. I moan around Darius' cock, and he hisses.

"Keep that up, Blaze." He grunts as he tears into my throat.

I feel a set of lips running along my stomach and judging by how gentle they are, it must be Zander. I begin to feel the tightening in my lower belly, and I grind into Blaze's mouth, trying desperately to find the friction. My pussy clamps and then his mouth is gone, my orgasm ebbing away again. Darius continues fucking my throat and I hear him chuckle when I growl in frustration. He's going to wish he didn't do that.

I relax my throat, and he pushes in further, then I clamp my teeth into his sensitive skin. Not hard enough to draw blood but hard enough to hurt.

"Fuck!" He squeals, the pitch so high, making me grin around his cock. "Stop!" He tries to pull back, but my teeth are pulling on his velvety skin.

The guys all stop touching me and I continue keeping my teeth clamped to Darius' dick.

"No more," Darius says with panic in his voice, "get her off."

"How do we do that?" Santos asks, "she'll take your boy with her, Bobbitt style."

"No!" Darius grits out and I chuckle around his softened cock, "make her fucking come."

"So, we're just going to give in to her now?" Blaze grunts, "you're giving her back all her power because she's lovingly biting your cock?"

"Oh yeah, asshole?" Darius snaps back, "let's switch spots."

"I'll do it," Santos offers, and I feel him move between my legs, "but it'll be my way, sweetheart."

My heart rate accelerates, and I can feel it thumping at my ribcage. His way means pain and blood. His way means I'm going to come harder than I have in a long time, probably since the last time he cut me open and used my own blood to defile me. His mouth attacks my clit and my own widens in a soundless scream, Darius' cock is released to his relief. I lean up on my elbows, staring down at Santos as he devours me, and my legs begin to shake, I need this.

"I almost lost it," I can hear Darius sniffle.

"They could sew it back." Zander says absently as he moves closer to where Santos is making a dessert out of my ass and pussy. "Tell me how she tastes."

Santos leans up and I growl at Zander for making him stop, reaching out to fist his shirt. I drag him into me just as I feel the sting on my inner thigh.

"I'm about to add some seasoning," Santos chuckles.

I release Zander who continues to crawl up onto the bed and begins to suck on my neck, but my eyes stay trained on Santos' fingers as he coats them in blood. Then he's pressing them into my pussy and pulling strange noises from inside me. He pumps them a few times and then pulls them out, smearing through the blood once more. This time his mouth lands on my clit and those bloodied fingers slip into my ass.

Stars fucking explode, my pussy clamps so fucking tight, and I get a strange sensation throughout my lower belly. I can't stop as it plows over me, and I feel the rush of wetness between my legs. It runs down between my asscheeks and along the fingers still lodged in my ass. A scream is trapped in my throat, and I can't seem to take in a breath. I collapse to the bed just as I feel Santos lining his cock up to my entrance.

My head is once again pulled down over the side and now it's Blaze standing there, his cock in his hand. His other hand wraps around my extended throat and he bends down into my face.

"You bite my dick, Reaper," his voice making me gasp just as Santos plows inside, "I will cut this fucking throat."

I believe him, nothing Blaze says should be taken lightly, and he always speaks the truth. I can feel Santos grabbing the slice on my thigh as he spreads my legs wider, and fucking slams into me over and over.

Then Blaze's wide cock is shoving into my mouth and down my throat, hitting deeper with each one of Santos' thrusts. I gag around him and struggle to breathe, the tears slipping from my eyes and dripping from my temples. Then a mouth latches to my clit as Santos is pumping into me and at first, I think it's Darius because of the proximity to Santos' dick, until I hear Zander.

"That does add seasoning." Zander moans and dives back down.

"Come on over here," I hear Santos say, "I've got a place you can put that."

I know he's talking to Darius and I'm relieved when Blaze cums down my throat, meaning I can watch what's about to happen. Blaze slips out and crawls onto the bed at my side, biting down on my nipple. I lift my head in time to watch Darius step behind Santos and push him forward, making him bend. I gasp when Darius coats his fingers through my blood then reaches behind Santos, prepping him with it.

"Oh fuck," I moan as I feel myself tighten again.

"You're fucking right, Reaper." Blaze chuckles, "you like watching that?"

I nod as I stare into Santos' face, seeing the moment Darius breaches him, and the mixture of pleasure and pain has me clenching again.

"I'm gonna come, again." I pant and fall back to the bed.

I can feel the erratic rhythm of Santos inside me and know it has everything to do with Darius being inside *him*. The thought pushes me over the edge just as I feel Zander nudging my mouth open. I open on a scream as my pussy clamps around Santos, but the sound is cut off as I'm stuffed with Zander's cock.

Holy fucking shit. This is way better than I thought it would be.

I plow into our girl harder as Darius pushes himself to the hilt in my ass, almost causing me to blow my fucking load instantly. No wonder Selene loves this shit.

I have no choice but to slow down for a moment, not wanting it to end so damn fast, but Darius is driving my senses into overload as he keeps a steady pace, my body clenching around him with every stroke. Fairly sure I died because nothing has ever felt so good before, and I'm definitely in Heaven. Better make the most of it, because the moment God realizes I'm at his big shiny gates, he's going to throw my ass back down to hell where I belong.

Look out, Satan, I'm on my way.

Darius grips my hip, kneading my flesh with his large hand and lets out a guttural groan that I've never heard before, drawing a similar sound out of Selene. I don't realize I've stopped moving until Darius swats my ass sharply, reaching around to grab my throat firmly.

"Move, or I'll have to fuck you so hard, I'll be fucking you into her too," he warns, my lips kicking up into a smirk.

"Don't threaten me with a good time. Are you trying to make me bust already?" I tease, but his eyes darken as I peer over my shoulder, his voice low.

"You asked for it."

I hardly have time to brace myself with Selene's hips before Darius picks up the pace, fucking me with so much force that he throws my body forward into Selene, a gasp leaving her in surprise.

Zander chuckles while pulling his dick out of her mouth, then dives down to claim her lips with his, swallowing her sounds as Darius continues to rail into me hard and fast, my balls becoming tight as he repetitively keeps hitting the right spot, and Selene's pussy gripping my dick like a vice.

I glance down to see the blood mixed with Selene's juices, my dick getting even harder if that's possible, and my fingers are digging into her slender waist so hard that I know for a fact, it will bruise. I love seeing my marks all over her pretty skin, and I can't help but pull one of her legs up higher to bite her calf muscle firmly, watching her reaction.

No girl has ever reacted like Selene does, and knowing she's willing to take everything I've got to give, makes my dick hard every time I think about it. I know I can always rely on Darius to make me feel good, but having Selene too? I'm the luckiest asshole alive.

I manage to get some sort of control over myself and start thrusting of my own accord, clenching my teeth, and trying hard to hold off on my release as Darius reaches around to cup my balls, rolling them firmly in his hand with a small bite of pain, causing my breath to become short and sharp.

"You don't get to cum until she does," Darius orders, making me growl.

"Then maybe stop making it feel so fucking good, holy fuck," I hiss as he slows down to deep, slow strokes giving me a second to recover. Blaze snorts but keeps his eyes on Selene as Zander kneels over her face, giving me a grin.

"I need lube."

Darius slows almost to a stop, most likely giving him the same look that I am. Zander isn't usually one to play our type of games, but the look in his eyes says otherwise.

"You want me to make some lube for you?" I ask darkly, groaning when he nods.

"Yep. I want to slide my dick between these beautiful tits," he answers. No sooner are the words out of his mouth, he's jumping almost right off the fucking bed, and Selene lets out a tired giggle.

"Stick your asshole in my face and expect me to lick it, big boy. You're lucky it wasn't a finger." She snickers.

"*You're* lucky it wasn't a finger," he snaps, giving me a look to hurry the fuck up. I quickly place another cut on her thigh close to the first one and squeeze around it, drawing more blood from below the surface as I rub my hands in it. I reach out to run one hand down the center of Selene's chest, leaving the sticky blood behind for Zander to use.

I press my hands on her stomach lightly, mesmerized by how pretty the bloodied prints look against her skin. She's mine. Ours. She was fucking made for us, and I must have done something good in a past life to deserve her.

Zander pushes her tits together, sliding between them with a groan and he watches himself fuck them slowly.

He's gritting his teeth and suddenly inhaling sharply. "Selene."

"It's just a tongue, you big baby," she mumbles, making a choking sound as he leans back to attempt to suffocate her with his balls.

"Fuck!" he barks and falls forward so far that if my dick weren't buried in our girl, it would have ended up down the back of his throat. "She stuck her finger in my ass!"

"I'm going to stick my dick in you in a minute if you come any closer," I chuckle, annoyance takes over his face as he leans back to glare at me.

"Try it, fuckface."

"That's Captain fuckface to you, peasant," I throw back, groaning as Darius slaps my ass harder than last time.

"Would you both shut the fuck up? It's just a finger, Zan. Lean back and let her blow your mind," he exclaims, thrusting firmly into me and making me hiss out a breath. My ass is getting tender, but I don't want him to stop. My boy knows I like it when it hurts.

I start fucking Selene like it's the last time I'll get to feel the warmth of her pussy, a strangled scream coming from her as she's muffled by Zander's balls, my fingers snaking between us to rub her clit furiously, pulling an orgasm from her out of nowhere.

The moment her body clenches around mine, Darius grips the back of my neck and fucks into me as deep as he can go, pushing me over the edge. I come so fucking hard that black spots dance in front of my eyes, and my body jerks as Darius keeps going without breaking pace.

"Jesus fucking Christ, man. Stop!" I force out as my fingers fist the bedding below us, my body pulsing even more as his dick draws out my release until I'm a pile of fucking jelly. He ignores me for a few more seconds before growling and burying deep, going still as he sinks his load inside me.

Selene's a panting mess, and she must be tired after that, because she leaves Zander's ass alone.

Once Darius and I collapse, Zander grins and moves so he can flip her onto her knees, having no choice but to hold her up as her arms and legs shake. I raise an eyebrow as I watch him cup her pussy, catching my cum and dragging it up to her ass, not hesitating before sliding his dick into the hilt.

It doesn't take him long to finish, and Selene's a sobbing mess by the time we all sprawl out to catch our breaths. Next time, I'm shoving my dick in Darius and giving that man the ride of his life. Holy fuck.

I have no idea why Santos decided today was the day he wanted me to fuck him, but I wasn't going to fight him on it. I've always wondered what his ass would feel like around my dick, and it didn't disappoint.

Selene's curled up between Daddy Blaze and Zander, Blaze murmuring threats into her ear and making her swoon like the pain junkie she is, while Santos happily snuggles into me, a light laugh leaving him as I drop an arm over his sweaty stomach.

"Fuck, D. My ass is pulsing like you're still inside me."

"Feel good?" I mumble with a smile, his abs tensing as my fingers move over the ridges, my dick stirring at knowing he enjoyed that as much as I did. I'm surprised it has any life left after that bomb-ass sex.

I don't think before grabbing his chin firmly and tilting his face up, dropping a lazy kiss on his lips and biting firmly into the plump flesh, a desperate groan leaving him instantly. One of his hands trails up my bare chest, his hand resting against my throat and tightening the smallest amount.

I hear Selene mumble something about us making her pussy wake up again, but I keep my attention on Santos, knowing he needs a second for me to center him. We shared a lot more than just sex, and I know it's the start of something more.

I'll need more than blow jobs from him from now on because holy fuck, that was hot.

He pulls back and peers down at me, a cheeky grin on his face.

"You do know your ass is mine next time, right? I'm going to fuck you so hard I'll cum in your throat."

"God, I hope so," I grin back, but Blaze gives us a dirty look as he props himself up on his elbow.

"If you two don't shut the fuck up, I'll fuck the pair of you so hard, you'll both snap into two pieces."

"Ooh, Daddy Blaze is mad," I chuckle, but Santos lets out a loud groan.

"You'd make it hurt so good, too. Spread my cheeks and spit in my ass first though, okay? I like to work up to the burn."

Blaze snarls and grabs a pillow, hitting Santos firmly in the face, but he just cackles in response. "A naked pillow fight? You naughty boy! How'd you know that was one of my kinks?"

"Would you fuckers knock it off?" Selene grumbles, her face presses into Zander's neck as she tries to snuggle into him more to escape our banter. Zander pulls her on top of him, wrapping his arms around her and not giving a shit that our cum is probably leaking out of her and onto his skin.

"Yeah, guys. Shut up so we can nap," he states, his fingers drawing patterns on her bare back and capturing my attention. Her skin is covered in dried blood, and the moment my dick springs to life, Blaze attacks me with the pillow, too.

"No more play time, you fucking heathen. Give it a rest already before one of us dies from a fucking heart attack," he snaps, but I snatch the pillow and give him a smirk.

"You don't think that hot little pussy is worth dying over? Dude, totally fucking worth it. Wanna go again, Selene?"

She moans, reaching a hand out to rest on Santos' chest.

"I can't move."

"You don't have to move, baby. I'll do all the work," I half joke, knowing if she says yes, I'll take her again. Santos mumbles his agreement, but he doesn't move either, giving me a nice big ego boost. It takes a lot to tire him out, and I seem to have succeeded. It's like unlocking an achievement on the Xbox. I'm cool as fuck.

I reach over Santos to run my hand over Selene's ass, but Zander slaps me away with a grunt.

"Leave her alone. She needs to rest, and we should probably feed her before she's hangry."

"I'll fucking feed her this monster cock in a second," Santos mumbles, but he's half asleep in the pillow. I laugh, poking him in the ribs with my finger.

"You're going to force feed her Daddy's dick? Kind of you."

"Don't fuck with me, you know I should really have a license for this weapon of cunt destruction," he chuckles, peeking at me and winking. Well, I'm pretty sure it's a wink. Hard to tell when half his face is in the pillow.

"Sure you do. Better get that sorted right away before someone arrests you," I deadpan, his eyes closing as he smirks.

"The only fucker alive that I'll let cuff me is right here, thank you," he murmurs as he falls asleep, and Blaze rolls his eyes at me as I grin. I'd be totally down for that.

I didn't realize how badly I needed a nap until I woke up hours later to find Blaze snoring beside me. Everyone else is missing. I sit up and rub my eyes, glancing around the room to find the bathroom door open and laughter coming from inside.

I swing my legs out of bed and pad towards it, pushing the door open more to step inside. I find Selene sandwiched between Santos and Darius in the shower as they wash the blood and cum from her skin. I lift the toilet seat and take a piss, glancing over my shoulder to sneak a peek at Selene. She is fucking stunning.

She raises an eyebrow when she catches me staring, her body arching into Santos as he dips down to suck a nipple into his mouth.

"If you piss on the floor, I'll rub your fucking nose in it. Do you want to come and join us?"

"I'm not a bad dog," I scowl. "And I think I've played with you three enough for a few hours." I can't believe I used her blood as titty lube. The way Santos and Darius play has always made me scrunch my nose up, it's not my thing, but fuck I was horny as hell watching them at work earlier. I knew I'd pussy out if I didn't just jump straight into it; I asked Santos to cut her for me before I could think about it any longer.

It felt kind of weird, the blood being warm and sticky unlike the lube I usually use, but my dick was more than happy to jump right into it, even with the sneaky wench prodding and licking at my ass. Won't lie, kind of felt good. I really have to stop spending so much time with Santos, his crazy must be rubbing off on me.

"You saying you've had enough of me, Zan?" she pouts, making me snort.

"No. If you want me to fuck you, I'll fuck you, but those two clowns can go find something else to do. There's only so much crazy I can handle in a day, and I'm at capacity."

I finish my piss and lean back against the sink, crossing my arms to watch them. Selene winces as Darius' fingers slip between her legs, her body tender from the pounding it took earlier, but she still leans into his touch like she can't get enough. No matter how bad it hurts, she won't run because our little hellcat craves the pain.

Surprisingly though, Darius doesn't shove his fingers inside her like I thought he would, he simply moves his fingers across her skin, washing away the evidence of our fun. Santos does the same with her breasts, grumbling about having to wash away his mark from her skin.

Big softies.

Blaze finally stumbles in, barks at everyone to hurry the fuck up, then he climbs in the shower the moment it's vacated. Grumpy piece of shit.

I don't bother to speak as I step into the shower too, ignoring the death glare from him.

"What the fuck are you doing?" he demands as he scrubs soap all over his chest.

"I smell and look like a fucking crime scene. We share a girlfriend, I'm pretty sure we can share a fucking shower without grabbing each other's dicks. You're not my type anyway," I reply, his face twisting into a scary smile.

"You're exactly my type. I do love having little bitches on my dick."

He scares me so much more when he's making jokes. Freaky asshole.

Chapter Nineteen

Selene

I slip on my boots and pull the brush through my hair a few times. "I'm starving." I moan, "I'm about to become a cannibal, Darius gave me a taste for human flesh."

He grabs his junk through his pants and pales, "we never speak of that again."

I throw my head back and cackle as Santos snickers, "she almost made a lifelike dildo out of you."

Darius continues to growl as I open the door, "let Blaze and Zander suck each other off, I can't wait anymore. I'm starving."

"Papi Loco should be back by now," Santos says as he and Darius follow me out the door, "but we should wait for Blaze and Zander before we talk to him."

"Agreed." Darius nods as his arm lands around my shoulders, hauling me into his body. "You wouldn't *really* hurt my love stick, right baby?"

"In a heartbeat," I tell him, "You put it anywhere near another girl and I'll have it off and down your throat. You ever hold back orgasms from me again, I'll cut it off and shove it up your ass."

"Babe…" he sputters as Santos hoots.

"I wouldn't laugh, dipshit," I sneer at Santos, "you'll be chewing on your balls if you ever torture me like that again."

He swallows hard and nods, "got it. But keep in mind, I will bleed you dry if you ever decide to run from me again."

"Deal." I smirk and we continue on our way to the front.

The place is filled more than it was earlier and way more than the night before. Looks like the full club is back home and I look around at the unfamiliar faces.

"Reaper!" I hear Loqi call out and I turn toward the sound with a groan, "hungry?"

"He knows the magic word!" Darius says and I snort.

Perc and Vico are sitting with Loqi, and I gather that they are his men, while the others are Papi's. Just an observation but I would put money on it, but not my next meal because I'm about to kill someone if I don't get fed soon. The three of us approach their table and when Loqi raises his hand, three chairs are added. I sit in the one directly across from him while Santos sits on my right and Darius on my left.

"Where are the other two?" Loqi asks with a grin.

"Showering my blood off themselves," I lean across as his smile grows larger, "together."

He tips his head back and his black curly hair flops with it as he laughs. "I think you should stay here with us, what do you need so badly in New York?"

Santos' fist hits the table, and he bares his teeth with a growl, he sounds like a fucking Pitbull. "Watch it."

Loqi's hands go up but the smile on his face grows, he likes fucking with my boys and pushing their buttons, I need to be the one that puts a stop to it. He places both hands on the table and leans forward, seemingly to say something to me, but I don't give him the chance. I grab his wrist and my knife is embedded into the wood between his fingers, nicking his skin along the way. Perc and Vico stand as do Darius and Santos, but Loqi raises his other hand, halting his men's movements.

"Listen Loqi," I get right up into his face, "I've been respectful, and my boys have been taking your shit in stride, but it stops now. Don't fucking push me any fucking further because I don't give a fuck who your daddy is, I'll gladly die after sawing your fucking head off."

He pauses and takes a good look in my eyes, his widening a fraction with what he sees. I know I'm unhinged and now he does too.

"I hear you," he nods slowly, "loud and clear."

I sit back in my chair, taking my knife with me, and with my eyes still trained on him, I lick his blood from my blade. Actually, maybe unhinged doesn't cover it but I don't think I need to reiterate a single thing, he's got the picture now. So do his men by the apprehensive look in their eyes, finally, a girl gets the respect she deserves.

"Now, did you say food? Because I wouldn't lie about that either."

"Yes," he stands up from his chair, "out back we have a grill going. Hamburgers, dogs, and shrimp." We get up and follow him out the back door, "grab a beer." He points to a cooler. Darius and Santos do just that, but I want to keep my wits about me.

We grab some burgers and hotdogs and then we follow Loqi to an empty picnic bench. I'm surprised his boys let him leave with us without them, but he looks at ease. I guess he should since the twenty plus men outside wouldn't hesitate to shoot our heads off.

"My dad's just resting right now, it was a long ride and he's old as fuck." Loqi says as he takes a swig of his beer, "soon he'll need me to take over."

"Watch your mouth," an older biker says from the table to our left, he's a mean motherfucker with a patch over his eye, and a long grey beard to match his long grey hair. "Papi would still bend you over his knee, boy."

"Yeah, yeah," Loqi waves him off, "that's Hook."

Santos chokes on his beer and stands up abruptly, "do you speak pirate?" He calls out and when Hook gives him an odd look, Darius hauls him back down to his seat.

"Have you lost it completely?" Darius chuckles and Santos glowers at the old man.

"Fucking scallywag." He mutters and gulps down his beer.

I begin to laugh and Loqi joins in just as Blaze and Zander wander outside, clearly looking for us. I watch as they're ushered over for food and when their plates are full, I raise my hand. They make their way over and sit down, digging into their food.

"Did you have a nice shower together?" Loqi asks sweetly and Blaze chokes on his food.

"It was nice, thank you." Zander says before he bites into his burger. I snort and Blaze cuts me a look of death. Sexy motherfucker.

"Where's the old man we need to talk to?" Blaze asks around a mouth of meat.

"See?" Loqi calls out to Hook, "they haven't even met him, and they know he's an old man."

"Probably from the shit you're spewing," Hook retorts.

"Papi is resting, apparently." I answer, doubt lacing my words.

I watch as a couple of guys begin throwing knives, the target is on the side of the building they threw me into when we got here. I watch closely and snort when one completely misses the target.

"They're going to kill someone," I jut my chin toward them.

"Those are our prospects," Loqi smiles wide, "maybe they need someone to show them how it's done." I know what he's insinuating, and I ignore him while I bite into my burger.

"Scout and Chance!" Loqi calls out, "we have a treat for you today."

"Are those real names?" Zander asks, looking shocked.

"Nope, those are the names we give every prospect. We take two at a time and when we recruit them, Papi changes their name."

"I see." Zander nods as Chance and Scout approach.

"Guys, I have a real treat for you today." Loqi rubs his hands together.

"No, you don't." I shake my head.

"Oh, come on, one shot at the target. Unless you're afraid you'll miss it?" Loqi sneers and I know what he's doing, trying to call me out like I'm an insecure man.

I bite the bait anyway, "fine, but you're the target." I stand up and pull my knife from the belt around my waist.

"What?" he gets a mischievous look in his eye. "You want to kill me?"

"Yes," I deadpan and then point to the bowl of tomatoes and onions, "but I'll settle for throwing a knife at the vegetable on your head." He lifts a brow and I chuckle, "unless you're scared."

A few of the guys sitting at the tables laugh and Santos snorts, "I wouldn't mind seeing that hilt sticking out of an eye socket."

My guys laugh at that and Loqi stands from his seat, "fine." He walks over to the table with the bowl of veggies and grabs an onion.

"*Oh, come on,*" I mimic him, "grab the tomato, make it lifelike."

Again, snickers circle the lot, and I can see a light blush stain his cheeks, I fucking bask in his embarrassment. He stands in front of the target with the tomato on his head and a taunting grin.

"Okay, Reaper-" He's cut off by the whir of my knife as it flies through the air, into the tomato, and slams into the center of the target, the tomato completely splattered on the wood like blood. Loqi hasn't moved and the lot falls completely quiet.

"Chance," I say without looking at either of the prospects, "grab me my knife."

One prospect runs to the knife embedded in the wood as Loqi finally blinks free of his shock. The lot begins to pick up, but I now have the attention of a few older men. Their curiosities make my stomach tighten; this is what I wanted to avoid. I don't want any interest lingering on me, because once I find out what happened to Jan, I'm out of here. I won't be taking on any Reaper jobs for any of them because that's what I'm expecting with their interest.

"Who trained you?" he asks.

"You wouldn't know him if I told you, but I mostly trained myself. Long hours practicing and daydreaming about my blade sinking into the people I wanted to kill."

"It's going to be hard to let such an asset go." He murmurs and it's honestly something I suspected would happen as soon as they found out who I was.

"I'm not your asset."

"But you could be," he nods as he guides me back to the table, "we need help. Skin trafficking here is at an all-time high, and assholes keep encroaching on our turf, selling their product." He looks to my guys for backup but each one of their faces stay blank. They would never agree to something without me.

"Look," I say as I lean on the table with both hands, "the skin trade is on the rise everywhere. I'm needed back home." The prospect comes back and hands me my knife, the blade red with tomato juice. "I wouldn't mind helping you guys if you actually helped me as well. Which you haven't yet. I was picked up like cattle and dragged into this compound. From the second I asked for my sister, you've been putting me off from talking to the one man that can apparently help me. Bad business."

He lets out an exasperated breath and scrubs his hand down his face, "what if we don't know where your sister is? What if she never came through here?"

"Then I'll be on my way to follow other leads. But I need to find out either way."

"What about if we paid you well for your services?" He begins grasping at straws.

"We don't need money." Money-bags Zander retorts and when a few of us snicker he raises a brow, "what? We don't."

"You heard him," I thumb at Zander, "we don't do this for profit, we do it to save people. If we made money from saving skin, then that would make us no better than the cunts that sell it."

The place falls quiet again and Loqi scratches at his head, "my sister was taken as well." He begins and I sit down for what will be his final sell, "She was twelve and we searched everywhere for her, but we failed. We never found her."

"How long ago was that?" I ask him.

"Seven years."

"With all due respect," I lean across the table, "mine has been missing a lot longer than that. I need to find my sister, my flesh and blood, before I help anyone else find theirs. Now, I'm sure you understand seeing as your own sister is missing."

"Okay, I hear you." He exhales and stands, "let's go talk to Papi and figure this all out."

"Thank you." I nod and stand to follow him. I feel the guys at my back, and I feel safe with them being so close. I chastise myself again for attempting to do this without them.

We're led through the main room they had the party in last night and Darius whistles when we see the mess. "Is that a used condom?" He points to what is definitely a condom, used or not, laying across a couch cushion.

"Yeah," Loqi chuckles, "never sit on those couches, the old men had them before us and they've been cum soaked for years."

"Charming." I mutter and Zander laughs as his arm snakes around my neck.

"Like you were earlier," he whispers in my ear.

"Watch it," I warn him, but I can't keep the smile off my face, "or I'll start talking about your daddy's big dick." He drops his arm with a grumble and Loqi turns to give us a questioning look, "I fucked his daddy first." I explain with a wink. He gives me an answering chuckle and continues to lead us down a narrow hallway.

"Stop telling people you fucked my dad." Zander mutters.

"Next time you talk shit, I'll tell them you both fucked me together."

Santos roars behind me and Darius joins in, "you just did baby." Darius says between chuckles.

"I guess I did." I wink again as Loqi looks between me and Zander. "I was the ham in that fat, juicy, club sandwich."

"Oh my god," Zander moans and covers his eyes with his hand. "Stop talking."

"Tons of mayo in that sandwich," Blaze pipes up and I look back at him in shock. He rarely joins in our fun, but I can see he likes torturing Zander.

"On both buns," I snicker and we both chuckle.

"Fuck you both." Zander moans and motions to Loqi to continue. "Let's get this over with."

"You're fucking freaky up there in New York," he whistles, "I wouldn't mind a ham sandwich with Henny if dad would let it." He shakes his head and leads us to a set of couches. "Chill here, I'll call him and see if he's done with his… uh… meeting."

"I'm not sitting on any of your couches." I shake my head, and he laughs.

"No one is allowed back here, much less get a chance to fuck on them. Papi would slit throats." Loqi motions for us to sit. "I'll be back." He disappears behind a door that has a large golden plaque reading, 'Vice President.'

We sit and Darius gets a naughty look on his face as he pulls me onto his lap. "Let's see if he can slit five throats though." My knees land on either side of his thighs and I ground down onto his hard cock.

Arms come around my waist and I'm lifted off, then settled on another lap. I turn to look over my shoulder and find a dark set of brown eyes looking at me irritated. "Sorry Daddy," I lean in and kiss the scar on the side of Blaze's face, "you know my weakness is cock."

His hand locks around my throat and I'm hauled back against his shoulder, "I do know that but ours will be the only cocks you'll have for the rest of your life, hooker. Understand? No more albinos or other hookers."

"Aniyah!" I exclaim and sit up in his lap.

"Yeah, that bitch." He grumbles.

"No!" I swat at his chest, "I'm supposed to find out about Aniyah today too. I'm a terrible friend, I got cock-stracted."

"Cock *what*?" Zander asks.

"Distracted by cock." I moan, "we need to find out where Aniyah is."

"Fuck her," Blaze grumbles and I swat him again. "She doesn't join us."

"She wouldn't want to." I roll my eyes, "but I still need to make sure she's okay."

Finally, Loqi comes out of his office, and I stand to face him, "where's Aniyah?" he cocks his head and looks confused, "one of the girls I was snatched with, she was really sick when we got here but I haven't seen her yet."

"Oh, the girl with the purple hair?"

"Yes!" I nod.

"She's back and in Medical, she had an overnight stay at the clinic, she was pretty dehydrated. But she's okay now."

My shoulders deflate and I feel immense relief, "thank you."

"No problem, we're not monsters." He grins and leads us to a door with an identical plaque to the one on his, only this one says 'President'. "He's ready for you now." Loqi opens the door, and we find who I would assume is Papi standing between a set of bare legs. The chick is engulfed by his size as she sits in front of him on the table. Even from the back, he's large and wide, stacked with muscle. "Man," Loqi whines, "you said you were done."

"We are done," Papi answers, his voice is so deep, and he has a bit of a Mexican accent. "I'm just saying bye to my woman."

His *woman* swats him on the arm, and I see her small delicate hand, it's adorned with rings.

"Shut up," she says, and the sound of her voice has my brows crashing together. Then I see her head pop out from the side of his body and I'm stunned in place. Pale blonde hair, bordering on white, pale white skin, and a dusting of freckles meet the hair line. My finger touches the few I have on my nose and remember I used to call them fairy kisses. Jan told me they were fairy kisses.

"Hey," her voice calls out to us, and my feet are stuck solid to the ground, I can't move. Her eyes are a dark shade of blue, looking nearly black, and she still has a ring in her left nostril. "I'll just get out of your hair." She smiles, her plush mouth widening with the motion and her straight, white teeth fucking sparkling. Papi doesn't let her move, and she giggles while she swats his chest.

"Wait a minute…" Blaze says as we all listen to her giggle and then his eyes land on mine.

I nod, "Jan." I say loud and clear into the room, and I hear her gasp. Her face appears again, and she pushes Papi aside. Everyone is watching as she hops off the table and stands in front of me. She's trembling and her hands land on her cheeks.

"It can't be." Her voice shakes as much as her body.

"I was told you were taken and possibly sold as a sex slave," I can hear the disdain in my own voice, "but clearly that wasn't the case. You built yourself a nice life here, humping the president of a biker gang no less."

"Selene?"

"Were you hit over the head or something when they grabbed you? You sound slow now." I snap. "Of course, it's Selene, the sister you left behind."

"I didn't leave you behind," she steps forward. "I couldn't ever do that to you."

My hand snaps to the handle of my blade, "don't come any closer or I'll fucking gut you."

"What?" Her eyes round and I hear a gun getting cocked in my direction, "no, Papi." She puts her hand out, "put it away." He listens to her and then she continues, "I was sold to a man named Henry Walton by our mother. She was apparently offering him sexual favors for drugs and when he came by our apartment, we were there. He wanted you but I refused and offered myself instead."

"So, you left me with her?" I snarl and watch as fat tears roll down her cheeks.

"Yes," she moans, "I thought I could break free and come back for you. But I couldn't and before I knew it, I was on my way to Nevada. I was sold around, and it was years before I was rescued by Papi and his MC." She looks at him fondly and then back to me, "I told him about my little sister, and he helped me come back to New York to find you. But when I went back to the apartment, it was empty, trashed, and blood was all over the couch."

"That's where I threw a knife into our mother's head." I growl and her eyes widen.

"I was told the place was robbed and everyone inside was killed." She continues to cry but it does nothing to soothe my anger. She was okay here and living her life while I struggled on my own. She was having the time of her life fucking the president of the MC while I was killing men, looking for her. While I risked my life, time and time again, she was safe here in Nevada.

I turn my back on her and stride out of the room, I can't even look at her right now.

"Wait! Selene!" She chases me into the hallway, "please I was told you were dead!"

"I was told you were probably dead too!" I scream and my voice echoes throughout the small space. I can see my guys standing behind her and then Papi and Loqi behind them, watching us and knowing not to interfere. "I was told this whole mission of finding you would be a waste of my time! But I did it anyway!" I take a deep breath, "Because if there was even the slightest chance that you were alive, I was willing to risk my life to find you!"

She drops to her knees and places her hands in a prayer position, "please forgive me for not trying harder."

I turn my back on her and everyone else. I don't want to be here. I storm off back the way we came, and I hear Zander's voice behind me.

"I'll take care of her."

I'm staring at the man they call Papi, and I can't seem to focus on anything else. I barely notice when Selene takes off with the biker bitch hot on her heels, or when Zander declares he'll take care of her. Everything else fades away as pain mixed with hope fills my chest.

No one seems to realize my silence, not that I'm surprised. Blaze lets out an impatient growl, giving us the side eye. "I'll go find them and make sure she doesn't kill the cunt."

"Watch your mouth, boy," Papi warns with a vicious growl, his attention on Blaze, allowing me more time to process my thoughts. I study him and Loqi while Blaze argues with the old bastard, the two of them nose to nose until Papi pulls a gun out and aims it at Blaze's head.

Blaze grins manically, but Loqi is the one who steps between them.

"Papi, stand down. Let him chase his girl."

"Why should I give a fuck about his whore?" Papi grits out, the grin slipping from Blaze's face, but Loqi continues.

"Why should they care about your girl? Just let the fucker go chase her down and we can all talk later. Now's obviously not a good time."

After a second of grumbling, Papi flicks his wrist towards the door, dismissing Blaze like a dog, and Blaze instantly takes the chance to leave and make sure Zander has everything under control. I hope he does, or we could end up in a rain of bullets trying to fight our way out if Selene snaps like I think she might.

Darius finally notices my silence, glancing over and brushing his hand across mine.

"Hey, you good?"

I keep staring at Papi until I can't take it any longer.

"Papi?" My voice is barely there, but the bastard looks at me with a scowl as if I yelled it.

"What? I have better things to do than stand around here jerking each other off," he barks, my eyes darting to Loqi for a second, his eyes a mirror of mine. I turn back to Papi, my voice stronger.

"Dad."

Darius curses under his breath, Loqi's eyebrows basically fly off his fucking face with how high they go, and Papi stares at me with confusion. His eyes flicker between Loqi and I, his brow creasing as he thinks.

"There's no way."

"I was a fucking kid when you left. Why the fuck did you leave?" I grit out, resentment filling my veins like poison. I am allowed to feel resentful, and it doesn't seem like he's all that happy to see me either.

Loqi is tense like me, and the moment Papi moves closer to inspect me more, I step back with a sneer. I always wondered what had happened to the man who abandoned me, but I guess it's easy to see why he did. He obviously had another family and another fucking son to raise.

"Santos?" he finally murmurs, my heart cracking a fraction before I can block it out. Would I have turned out a different man if he'd stuck around? I eye Loqi and hold back a snort. Obviously not. Loqi has a lot of similarities to me, particularly his violent streak and his smart mouth.

"San?" Darius says softly, taking my hand and giving it a squeeze. "You wanna go?"

I am stuck between wanting to hug Papi and kill the bastard. Papi's eyes drop to our hands, but I don't pull back. If he has a problem with it, I'll gun him down where he fucking stands, not giving a shit about the consequences.

"My boy!" Papi exclaims, a big grin taking over his face as he suddenly embraces me in a hug, weakening the walls I've built around my heart even more. I stand there stunned for a moment, before my arm goes around him and I hug him back, not letting Darius go.

Loqi is frozen like stone, confusion filling his gaze as he watches us, and I have no idea what he's thinking. Something weird tugs inside me as I realize I have a brother. A brother that I want to murder every time his eyes run over my baby girl. Blood doesn't make him family, not yet. Selene comes first in every aspect.

"Look at you! So grown up!" Papi states happily as he steps back, glancing at Loqi with excitement. "Loqi! This is your brother, Santos!"

"We've met," he grunts, still not jumping on board with the family reunion. I don't blame him; I don't particularly give two shits about him right now either. Papi inspects Darius next, noticing my hand tightening around him at his scrutiny.

"The fuck's this?" he asks, disgust rolling off him. Darius goes to speak, but I cut him off bluntly, my voice sharp.

"Touch him and I'll kill you. He's mine."

The ghost of a smile plays on Darius' lips, and Papi snorts.

"You can try, boy. Thought you were with the crazy chick? Real men don't like a dick in their ass."

"Real men love whoever the fuck they want," I grit out, his eyes filling with amusement as I continue. "They're both mine."

"I see. How's your Ma?"

"None of your business," I bark, his eyes narrowing.

"Don't use that fucking tone with me, I was just asking."

"Well, don't. How about we talk about Jan? Or the fact that you never came back for me?" I demand, his face scrunching as if in pain.

"Your ma made it clear that I was to stay away from you after I left. She didn't want some good for nothing asshole near her kid. If I was leaving, she didn't want me to come back. Henny is none of your business either," he mutters, making me snort.

"We came here expecting to find *Henny* hurt or dead. Is she really here of her own free will? Is this saving women mission some bullshit front to get away with other shit? I don't believe that you found it in your heart to save women after you abandoned yours."

He snarls and gets in my space, anger pulsing through him in waves.

"Watch it. You don't get to disrespect me in my fucking territory. You've seen the women around here, and they're fucking fine. I might be the biggest bastard alive in your eyes, but I'm not. I do what I can to help those women because they don't deserve to have their lives stripped away by a heavy hand. They don't deserve to be scared and used until they have nothing left. I'll kill any man in cold blood, but never a fucking woman," he spits, his teeth grinding at my accusation.

I know he's right, and at the end of the day I honestly have no idea who the man in front of me is, but that's on him for leaving me.

Santos is going to explode and massacre everyone soon; I can sense it. Watching his stand-off with his father isn't something I had scheduled on the fucking calendar this month, that's for sure.

Loqi looks just as fucked up as Santos right now, not that I blame him. This conversation took a turn that none of us expected, and now all I care about is making sure we get out alive and Santos doesn't start stabbing anyone. Killing the Pres. might not be a good idea, just saying.

I tug Santos back a step, allowing him more room to breathe. He doesn't cope well with being backed into a corner, believe it or not. He's tense, and I want to kiss the tightness from his jaw before he breaks a tooth, but I don't think now is a good time to show him affection. I don't feel like a punch in the guts.

"Nice piece of ass you got. Where'd you find her?" Papi smirks, knowing he's pushing buttons. I'll kill him before I let Santos do it, because that split decision would haunt him for the rest of his life.

"She's not a piece of ass," I bite out, Papi raising an eyebrow as he turns to me.

"Oh, you speak. Was starting to think you were mute." Asshole.

My hand rests lightly on Santos' lower back to calm him, my fingers creeping up under his shirt a little to soothe him. I hate not knowing what's going on inside his head right now, but either way he's either murderous or hurting. I don't like that.

"This shit between you two has nothing to do with me, but our girl does. Don't disrespect her," I answer, focusing on the feel of Santos' skin under my fingertips. He can talk shit about me all he likes, but not Selene.

I turn to Loqi with a scowl. "You honestly knew nothing about this?"

"I didn't know he fucking existed," Loqi glares back, causing Santos to tense even more. Great, now I've made it worse.

Santos laughs dryly, shaking his head slightly as the bitterness leaks into his tone.

"Why am I not surprised? Of course, you never mentioned me, I was the kid that you didn't want. Were you having an affair behind Ma's back? Knocked some bitch up and figured that kid meant more to you? He looks like he's my age, which means you were with Ma when he was created."

"It's not like that," Papi growls, but I'm quite sure he's full of shit by the way Loqi flinches. It's not obvious, but I see the slight jerk of his hand. This conversation is going nowhere good, that's obvious.

"Then why the fuck didn't either of us know about the other? Why did you keep us a fucking dirty little secret?" Santos hisses, but he leans back against my touch, my fingers pressing more firmly into his skin.

"It's my dick, I'll stick it where I want," Papi smirks cruelly, confirming he was full of shit a second ago. He cheated on Santos' mother, and he doesn't give a shit about the outcome.

Santos' fists clench by his side, and I reach up to grab his jaw in my hand, forcing him to look at me. He looks ready to punch me, but it wouldn't be the first time.

"He's not worth it," I say gently, his jaw loosening a little as his eyes soften. He stares at me for what seems like hours before taking my hand from his chin and holding it again, centering himself like I'd hoped he would.

Papi scoffs, giving me a dirty look. "You're a pair of filthy cunts. You like poking shit up his ass with your pin dick?"

"No need to sound threatened. Baby daddies who abandon their kids aren't my type," I throw back, hating that he's trying to make what we have sound like a pile of trash. I hope that Zander and Blaze are having a better time dealing with our little firecracker, and I hope none of this shit ends in a blood bath.

Selene storms into our room and I follow close behind, shutting the door. She strides into the bathroom and slams the door behind her when I hear a frantic knock on the door. I know who it is, and I wait a few moments before I open the door a fraction.

"Please, can I talk to her?" Jan asks, her face is blotchy red and swollen, but there's no mistaking that her and Selene are sisters.

I look over my shoulder and groan, "she's really angry and I can't be responsible if she throws a knife at your head."

She nods emphatically and I let her in just as the shower starts. She looks at the door and then back to me, I shrug, "you can wait here until she's done."

"Okay," she sits on the small chair in the corner, "tell me what she's like."

"She's fucking crazy," I shake my head and she laughs.

"She always was."

"She's a killing machine and she's known as the Reaper Incarnate."

"I've heard of that vigilante, but they say it's a man." She whispers shockingly.

"I assure you she's a woman." I grin and she cringes.

"I made her into that."

"No," I feel my irritation begin to rise, "she made herself strong and she did it *for* you. Don't you dare take credit for what she's become."

"I wasn't taking credit-" she begins but she's cut off by the sound of my girl singing her heart out in the shower, "dear god, it's gotten worse." She says as she looks towards the bathroom, "it was bad when she was a kid, but that sound is atrocious."

"Yeah, she can't sing worth a shit." I chuckle.

"I have a friend named Sammi and she was taken the same time I was, she likes to sing too, especially when she gets to drinking." She smiles fondly, "it reminded me of Selene."

Blaze opens the door then and strides inside, slamming it behind him.

"How could you give up on her?" He snaps and it sets off another round of crying.

"You don't understand, I thought it was the end, I had no family, and I was young." She sobs.

"Selene was young too when she began chasing down drug dealers to find information on her sister," Blaze takes a menacing step toward her, "when she picked up a knife and began to learn how to use it to defend herself," another step and he's towering over her, "when she started to sell her body to track down the men that took her sister away."

The water shuts off in the shower and Blaze continues to glare down at a sobbing Jan, she's definitely a lot softer than Selene. Selene would've had her knife in his balls already.

"I just want the chance to talk to her," Jan sniffs.

"I'll let it happen if that's what she wants, but you better understand you don't deserve it," he bends down until they are eye to eye, "you don't deserve her."

His words are harsh, but I agree with every single one of them and it's Blaze's nature to be cruelly honest.

"I know." Jan whispers.

"If you hurt her any more than you already have, please keep in mind that I'm a hunter, and I will enjoy the fuck out of hunting you down."

She nods and I haul Blaze back as the bathroom door opens. Selene sees us first and even though a naughty grin coats her sexy lips, her eyes are sad.

"Are you two here to make me feel better?" She husks out and my cock is ramrod hard.

"No," I swallow thickly and give her a slow once over, "Jan is here and wants to talk." I step out of the way and reveal her sister.

"My name is Henny now." She says as she stands. "I couldn't stand being Jan anymore."

"Felt guilty, did you?" Selene states as she drops her towel and begins to dress.

Blaze curses under his breath and I stand transfixed, I can't get enough of her.

"Yes," she nods, "I thought I failed you when I found out you were dead, and I hated myself. I hated Janelle."

Henny gasps when she sees the tattoo that takes up Selene's entire back, a menacing looking Reaper, and its large scythe that stretches from shoulder to shoulder. Selene sits on the bed and flips her knife back and forth, making me nervous for the other woman in the room. If she kills the president's old lady, we might as well kill ourselves, too.

"I knew that my greatest wish was to find you alive," Selene says, "but it was also my greatest fear." She turns to look at her sister, "because that would mean you left me behind to suffer with *her*." She must be talking about her mother.

"Not purposely."

"I know that, too. That's why I always convinced myself that if you were alive, you were being held against your will. So, imagine my shock when I find you giggling in the arms of a biker like you didn't just wipe your past out and me along with it."

Fuck. That hit me in the chest and I'm not even the one that forgot her.

"I would've never wiped you out if I thought you were alive," Henny tentatively sits beside her on the bed, "there was so much blood, Selly."

Selly? Oh, hell no, our girl ain't no Selly.

"The fuck did you just call her?" Blaze growls and I mentally give him props. "That's fucking disrespectful. She's a fucking warrior, call her by her proper name, *Henny.*"

I remind myself to buy the scary fucker a drink later because everything he's saying is honestly how I'm feeling.

"I'm sorry." Henny drops her head, "it's all I can say at this point."

"Thank you," Selene says as she stands and pulls on a shirt, the Reaper slowly getting covered, "I can thank you at least, because if you did continue to look for me, you would've found me, easily." She turns to look at her sister and a slow evil grin slides along her mouth, "and I wouldn't be who I am today."

Henny stays quiet and the room falls silent around us.

"You can head on back to your man now." Selene tells her.

"You hate me." Henny says as she stands.

"No, you're my sister, I'll always love you." Selene opens the door, "I just need some space and time. I just need you out of my face, really." Henny walks out slowly, and Selene slams the door at her back, "can you believe this shit?"

Blaze and I look at each other then back at her, both of us waiting for the bomb to slowly tick down to zero. But it doesn't happen. She puts her belt back on and slips the knife inside then looks at us expectantly.

"Where's Santos and Darius?"

"We chased after you." Blaze answers and she tsks.

"If that Papi Crazy motherfucker hurt my babies, this place is burning to the fucking ground, and it can take its precious *Henny* with it." Okay, so she's still mad and that ticking bomb may just explode if there's even the tiniest scratch on either Santos or Darius.

She yanks open the door and once again she's off with Blaze and I following her.

"How often are we going to have to chase this one down?" he growls.

"Forever, my man." I clap his shoulder.

Forever is a long fucking time.

I stare at her back as she strides down the hallway, her damp blonde hair swinging behind her, and her head held so fucking high and proud. Yeah, I guess I could do it forever, for her. I don't know when that happened, my willingness to chase this one woman, and my need to claim her, but it happened and now she's stuck with me. I don't even care that she wants the other three too, it makes my life easier actually because the four of us weren't ever going to split up.

Now we have a fifth and she's never splitting from us again, she completes us. I know I sound like a wet pussy, but it's true, Selene was made for us. I look over at Zander and the fucker has the same look in his eyes. We're all fucking crazy about the girl, and it makes me feel good, but also a bit apprehensive.

I was raised to believe that nothing good stays, eventually good feelings; people; and places disappear; and all that remains are the bad. So, I can't help but worry about the things that could happen. What if she falls out with one of us? Does she then fall out with all of us? What if one of the guys decides they're ready to move on? What happens to the rest of us? What if Darius and Santos decide they'd rather just be together? Will she leave all of us?

We step inside the main room and Selene looks around; her shoulders are tense. I can feel myself gearing up for a fight and I check that I still have my knife on my belt.

"Selene?"

I turn at the sound of a female's voice and groan when I see it's the hooker bitch.

"Aniyah!" Selene exclaims and rushes to her friend. Friends sound too casual after they've eaten each other dry, but whatever. "How are you?"

"They really took good care of me," she smiles but I can see she's still weak. She looks over at me and her eyes widen in recognition. "You know him?" She points to me, and Selene looks over her shoulder.

"Yeah, he's one of my guys." She turns back to Aniyah just as I run my thumb along my throat. Zander chokes on a laugh as Aniyah pales. "Why?"

"I thought he looked familiar," she visibly swallows. "Never mind."

"There's someone else with a large scar running down the side of his face in Nevada?" Selene stands with her hand on her hip, "looking as angry as this asshole?" She thumbs over her shoulder.

"I was stalking you for a while," I stare at Aniyah as I speak, "maybe she saw me then."

"Must be it." Aniyah looks away but Selene continues to flick her gaze between us.

"If I find out you two fucked, I'll circumcise you both," she walks over to me and stands on her toes, bringing her mouth closer to my ear, "twice." I shudder at the mental image and know she fucking means it. Which means if Aniyah is gonna speak, I'll need to shut her up, and permanently.

"That must be it." She shakes her head. "My mind is all over the place at the moment."

Selene walks back to Aniyah and settles on the couch beside her, leaning in close to speak.

"You fuck her?" Zander asks.

"She sucked my dick." I shrug and Zander laughs.

"You're getting cut a few inches."

"No, I'm not." I look at him, "if that bitch talks, I'll cut out her tongue."

Zander chuckles as he heads to the bar and I follow behind him, making sure to make eye contact with the little hooker one last time. I hope the look in my eye conveys my murderous intent if she is even thinking of talking.

"Licker," Zander hits the bar, "we need two glasses of your best Scotch."

"Coming up!" Licker nods.

"I do like it here," Zander muses as he leans his back to the bar.

"I don't." I grumble, "it's too fucking hot all the time, and here in this compound, people are deranged."

"Do you even know your friends?" He asks me.

"I'm used to you fuckers, and Selene? She's mine." I shrug, "it's different."

"Do you love her?" Zander asks quietly, we watch as both her and Aniyah get up to walk outside.

I watch her closely, the way her body moves, and the energy she puts off. A confident but psychotic attitude that's begging any motherfucker to test her.

"Yeah," I watch her until she disappears, "I think that's what this feeling is."

"Like you would do anything for her?" He muses.

"Like I will kill her if she fucks this all up." I correct him and he laughs. "Do you love her?"

"Yeah," he nods. "No question."

"So like, do we tell her? And then what? Get married or something?" I screw up my face at the prospect.

"We should tell her, but getting married is a little weird, no?" he raises a brow at me, "Can you imagine it? 'Hey priest! Can you hurry up with the vows, all of us need to get out of here and fill every one of her available holes.'"

I choke on my Scotch and roll my eyes at him. Accurate though.

Both of our heads snap up when we hear a loud crash and Santos' yelling.

"What the fuck was that?" Zander slams down his glass.

"Came from down that hallway," I point ahead and it's the one with Papi Loco's office.

"You have your knife?" he asks as he checks the gun in his holster.

"Yeah."

"Let's go." He darts forward and I hang back to look for Selene.

I don't know where the fuck she went, and I can't waste time looking for her. I chase after Zander and hope she doesn't castrate me for it later.

REAPED

Chapter Twenty

Selene

Aniyah still looks a little pale and I can see her struggling to focus. I know she was really sick, but I'm still worried about her.

"Are you sure you're feeling fine?"

"Yeah, it's just so loud in here," she gives me an apologetic smile. "I'm not used to this many people."

"I know what you mean," I nod and look around the room. "They're like one big family."

"I like it, but it'll take some time to get used to."

"Are you planning on staying?" I stare wide eyed at her.

"I'm thinking I might," she exhales. "There's nothing in Nevada for me now." She looks sad. I know she's thinking about her fake friendship with John.

"Colleen will miss you." I tell her with a nudge of my shoulder.

"On your way back," she grabs my hand, "could you pop in and tell her I'm doing good?"

"Yeah, I will."

She wipes her hand over her brow, and I begin to worry all over again, "do you want to go outside for a breather?"

"Yeah," she nods, "that'll be nice."

We head outside and I can feel the heat from Zander and Blaze's watchful eyes. I know a part of them will always be afraid that I'll run again, but they'll get over it eventually because I've learned my lesson. I need them.

"So, those are your guys?" Aniyah asks as we sit at one of the picnic tables in the lot.

"Yeah, that's two of them," I grin, "we're a hot fucking mess, but shit, I think I love them."

"Whoa," her eyes become saucers, "four?"

"Yep." I grin and I must look like a maniac. "All fucking four of them."

"Did you find anything out about your sister?"

My heart sinks with the thought of Jan - *Henny* - and I scrub my hand down my face, "she's here."

"Really?"

"Yep, she's the president's old lady," I chuckle at the fucking irony of it all. "She was here the whole time."

"I'm glad you found her." She smiles and pats my hand.

"I'm not so sure I am." I admit, "I was looking for an enslaved woman or a body."

"Then you must be happy she's alive and happy!" She exclaims.

"That just means she abandoned me, doesn't it?"

"Oh." She breathes with the realization and the air around us hangs heavy with silence.

"I don't know what to do now." I admit and stare down at my fingers.

"You forgive, Selene." She leans across the table, "you must forgive, if not for her, then do it for yourself."

"She didn't even try to look for me," I slam my fist on the table. "If I were truly dead, where would I be buried? Who were the witnesses? Cops must have reports, right?"

She nods along, agreeing with all my points, "yes. All of that is true. But was she the type," she taps her head, "to think of all that during a stressful moment?"

"If you're asking if she is smart, I would say yes, extremely. She's fucking the top old dog here, smart as a whistle."

Aniyah tips her head back and those purple curls bounce as she cackles. "I guess she is, huh?" She says as she wipes the tears from her eyes. "But listen," she continues after she calms down, "not everyone is as resourceful as you are. You are street smart, and you have investigation skills a detective would die for. That doesn't mean she's like that."

"I know but-"

"Did you also consider what she went through before getting here?" She cuts me off, "she was also taken, right? And I would assume, abused in every way imaginable. Maybe, she still had a victim's mentality and not yet a survivor's one. Maybe, when she heard you were dead, she couldn't see any other option anyways."

Her words dig into my stomach and settle next to my blackened soul. I never did consider what she went through before landing here with the Dientes Afilados. I was just thinking of myself and my pain.

"Thank you." I whisper as images assault me of what I've seen and heard happening to young ladies and children. It happened to my sister and instead of being happy she survived; I could only think of myself.

"Forgive her." Aniyah stresses. "She's your only family."

I lay my forehead on the table and take a deep breath; Aniyah's fingers smooth over my strands. I will forgive, I think I already have but I just need time to stop being so fucking angry. If I hadn't spoken to Aniyah, it would've lasted a lot longer than this.

"Hey," her voice breaks me out of my thoughts, and I lift my head. "That guy has been out there watching us the whole time." I look to where she's pointing, and my breath gets lodged in my throat.

"I know him." I stand and stare back at the man casually standing against a familiar Rolls Royce.

"Like a *good* know him?" Aniyah stands and asks cautiously.

"He's not a threat," I wave her off. "Sit here and I'll be right back."

"Okay," she sounds unsure but sits back down.

I walk toward the front gate and notice he's across the street, just watching like a fucking creeper. I stop in front of the prospect guarding the gate and point to the guy.

"Did you not find that weird?" I raise a brow. "Which one are you?"

"Chance." He says and then shrugs, "he asked for you but told me to wait until you were done with your conversation."

"Open the gate."

"Are you sure?" he looks around, "you shouldn't go out there alone."

"Don't make me ram my fucking foot up your ass while I yank my knife out of your skull." I growl.

"Fine." He shakes his head and opens the gate.

I stroll across the street, shielding my eyes from the early evening sun, and stopping a few feet in front of him.

"Mr. Walton's driver," I chuckle, "what the hell are you doing all the way down here in Nevada?"

"I work for Zander now," he smirks. "The new Mr. Walton."

The way he says that makes my stomach feel like it's filled with crawling cockroaches. Zander *is* the new Mr. Walton.

"The prospect told me you wanted to speak to me, what's up?"

"Mario's has a bomb pineapple and sausage pizza that I can never get enough of, it's all I've lived off for practically two years." He's smirking but I don't fucking get what he's saying.

"Nice." I nod slowly. Maybe he has developmental issues?

"You gave me their number when I asked for yours." He explains, his smirk still firmly in place.

It feels like ages ago when that happened, and I can't control the bark of laughter that escapes my mouth. "Sorry," I shrug. "I had my hands full with the first Mr. Walton."

"And now with the second, right?" he winks.

The words are meant to be funny, something to snicker at, but something is telling me that he didn't mean it as any joke, more like a snide comment.

"Fucking right." I nod, but it's tight and my smile is strained. Something is off. "You came all the way here to pick us up?" I raise a brow.

"I came to deliver something he asked for," he shakes his head and opens the back door. "And I was told not to bring it on a plane."

Oh, that sounds legit, but something is still off. "And you asked for me because?"

"I saw you sitting there, and it was easier than making some kid run around looking for Zander." Again, sounds legit.

"Hand it over then." I hold out my hand.

"Not that easy," he chuckles, "I can't let this be seen, I couldn't get on a fucking plane. Understand?"

So, it's illegal. My instinct is telling me to back away and go get Zander, but my pride is saying I could handle this douche.

"Get in and I'll sit in the front like I'm taking you somewhere." He says, "then I'll hand it over and you'll get out."

"Fine." I get into the backseat, and he shuts the door, climbing into the driver's seat.

"Reach under the seat." He tells me, keeping his eyes on me, reminding me of all the times he drove me to Henry.

I do what he says, but I can't feel anything. "There's nothing here." I snark.

"Further back," he says, and I bend down further, trying to see under the seat. "Mack is so excited to see you."

"What?" Before I can lift my head, something hard slams into the back of it and the world goes dark.

I'm two seconds away from beating Papi to a pulp. If it weren't for Darius gripping the back of my shirt in his fist, I probably would have dived at the fucker already. I'm not fucking gay; I just know what I have with Darius makes me feel good. What's so wrong about that? I bet the piece of shit just needs a big dick up his ass to loosen him up a little. Prick.

"Obviously, your mother failed at raising you. No son under my roof would accept any man's touch," Papi spits, giving Loqi a dark look. "Right?"

Loqi snorts, not seeming bothered by me fucking guys, and that's the only reason I haven't punched his lights out. Papi on the other hand is about to lose some teeth.

I take an angry step forwards, but a chick with purple curls runs in looking panicked, her eyes seeking mine out as if I'd do shit for her. I don't know who the fuck she is, and I don't want any other woman to think they're worthy of my attention.

Before I can shout at her to fuck off, she stops in front of me and speaks.

"Selene just got in someone's fucking car and left."

Anger and pain course through me as I stare down at the purple headed cunt, my heart aching. What if Selene has run again? Had her sister caused her to flee?

"Who the fuck are you? And what the fuck do you mean by that?" I snap, not meaning to take my mood out on her, but needing to vent it somewhere before I kill someone. I won't cope if Selene runs from us again.

"I'm Selene's friend Aniyah and she said you are all her guys. She just got in the car with this guy, and they left. He was waiting at the gate for her, and she went out to him," she answers, making Darius frown.

"Why the fuck would she go outside the gate alone?"

"Selene said she knew him. He had a flashy car and they seemed to be relaxed. I haven't seen him before though," she states as if that's fucking helpful.

I grab a nearby chair and throw it hard across the room, smashing empty beer bottles off the desk in the process. Footsteps pound towards us, and I get ready to face down with the piece of shit bikers, but Zander and Blaze run in with wide eyes.

"What the fuck?" Zander growls when he realizes it's me having a tantrum, as he'll call it. I go to throw a fist at Papi to remove some of my pent-up anger, but Loqi's hand darts out of nowhere and grabs my wrist, standing between us with a stern look. "Don't."

"You want to fucking fight me?" I snap, but his lip quirks up into a playful smirk.

"Not today. Trust me, don't do this here."

Aniyah steps back from me, not wanting to get hurt in the crossfire.

"Should I have stopped her?"

"Has all that purple shit in your hair fried your brain? Of course, you should have!" I yell, wanting to strangle the life out of her. I can't believe she let her get in a random car and drive off. I've lost her again.

Before I can say fuck it and punch Loqi in his stupid face, Darius fists my hair and tugs my face around to look at him.

"She didn't leave you."

"You don't fucking know that!"

He goes to speak but I slam my fist into his jaw, making him stumble back a step. He doesn't seem fazed; he simply moves in front of me again with determination.

"Babe, whatever happened, she didn't run again. I just know," he murmurs, my anger becoming distracted by him calling me babe. My body tingles at the sound, and I can't help but run my fingers across his jaw where I'd hit him.

"How do you know that?" I ask, sounding desperate but not giving a shit. If there's any chance that she has run, I'll be devastated and I'll probably kill her when I catch her again.

"The fuck are you talking about? Where's Selene?" Blaze asks in a low voice, Zander's eyes on us in question.

I give Aniyah a dark look while answering. "Selene got in some fucker's car and left. She told Aniyah she knew them."

It's silent for a second, other than Papi's chuckling. He's finding everything so fucking funny.

"You let her fucking go?" Blaze demands, his eyes on Aniyah with the promise of violence.

Aniyah cowers from Blaze as he glares at her, his hands flinching by her sides as he gets ready to kill her. Zander steps between them, his eyes on her.

"Did you get a good look at them? Did she mention who it was?"

"No, she just said she knew them. The windows on the car were tinted, I'm sorry," she breathes as if he's saved her. If Blaze wants her dead, he'll bowl Zander out of the way in the process. Once Blaze loses it, that's the end of it.

I know Selene wouldn't leave us here, she's made it clear that she understands what would happen if she did. I'm worried about her, but I'm just as worried about Santos. I can't handle him beating my ass daily again to burn down his pain.

He looks defeated as his eyes remain on me, looking at me as if I have the answer to everything. I don't, but satisfaction rolls through me at knowing the power I hold over him. I'm his anchor, and I always have been.

I have no idea where Selene is or where she's going, but it can't be good if she didn't think to tell us first. If she's just going to be gone ten minutes, she still would have told us.

Zander and Blaze are grilling Aniyah about the car, Santos is still staring at me with a broken heart, and Papi is grinning as if it's the best day of his life.

"Guess you boys were just a piece of ass to her after all." I'm going to kill him.

Santos jerks out of his staring contest with my face, swinging around to punch the bastard, but I haul him back and wrap my arms around him, wheezing as his fist jabs me in the ribs firmly.

"Let me go!"

I don't. I hold him tight enough to make sure he stays in one piece, my voice quiet.

"I can't lose you. Stop."

He goes limp in my arms, his forehead dropping to mine as his eyes fill with agony.

"I can't lose her again."

"We haven't. She's our girl, so let's go get her," I reply, a sudden calm washing through him.

"Right now?"

"Right now. Let's go."

Papi scowls, stepping in front of the open doorway. "You're not leaving yet. We have shit to discuss."

Santos takes my hand, surprising me as he remains calm. "We have nothing to talk about Papi. Get the fuck out of my way."

I have no idea what the old bastard sees in Santos' eyes, but after a second his features soften, and he steps out of the way.

The four of us leave the office, and I glance back to find Loqi watching us go.

"See you soon," he states casually, making Santos snort.

"Don't fucking count on it."

I know we'll see them again, because even if Santos is pissed today, he'll be curious and demanding answers tomorrow. He's spent his entire life chasing the ghost of his father, so I know it's not the end of their conversation. Not by a long shot.

We head back to our room and gather up anything of ours, not wasting time as we head out to our car and climb in. Blaze slams the door and starts the engine, a dark grin taking over his face.

"Let's go get our girl."

If anyone's hurt her, there will be hell to pay. No one fucks with our family.

Fucking no one.

Epilogue

Selene

I'm being moved as the ground underneath me swerves, my body rolls and hits metal. I open my eyes but it's dark, I have cloth stuffed in my mouth, and my hands are tied behind my back. I've learned how to get out of being tied up a long fucking time ago. I bend my body back and work my hands lower until they slip over my feet. I turn onto my back and reach for my belt, feeling my knife still tucked into it. Thank God I got this made.

I pull out the knife and carefully cut away at the thin rope. What a dumb fuck this asshole is. I get my hands free and pull the cloth out of my mouth. I could work the knife into the trunk's lock and open it, but where would the fun be in that? No, I think I'll just stay here and wait to see where the fuck he's taking me. I slip my knife back into the belt and slip my hands under my head, feeling the bump there with a wince. That fucker is dead when I get out of here. I rest on my hands and begin to whistle. I begin with the tune *She'll be coming 'round the mountain when she comes* and when I decide I like it, I put that shit on loop.

"I'll be stabbing some motherfuckers when I get out," I sing, "I'll be stabbing some dirty cunts when I get out. Stabbing motherfuckers, I'll be stabbing motherfuckers, I'll be stabbing dirty cunts when I get out. I'll be cutting off some dicks when I get out, I'll be cutting off some dicks when I get out. Cutting off some dicks, I'll be cutting off some dicks, I'll be cutting off some dicks when I get out."

The car lurches to a stop and I huff in annoyance, I was just getting to the good part. The rage begins to settle in, and I feel the energy course through my muscles. He must've thought he got one over on me, that he's a big strong man, and he accomplished tying me up and throwing me in a trunk, all while I was passed the fuck out. Big man. I begin to whistle again and when the trunk pops, I can hear his footsteps crunching over gravel. I whistle louder and then the crunching stops, making me grin.

"Oh, come on, big man." I taunt, "you got me in here… now, come get me out."

He's hesitating, so not completely stupid, and then his foot kicks open the trunk. I continue to lay there and when his head comes into view, I grab his hair. I haul myself up and slam my head into his nose, laughing as he screams. I jump out of the trunk and I'm laser focused as I grab my knife out of my belt. He doesn't see me as he's bent forward and gripping his nose. I grab his hair and lift him up, stabbing my knife through his left eye. Dropping him once he's dead.

I hear the cock of a gun and I finally lift my head to see four thugs standing in front of me, all of them with guns out.

"Oh, come on guys," I prop my bloodied hand on my hip, "I already got enough holes for everyone, I don't need anymore."

"She doesn't recognize us, boys." I hear a familiar voice from behind the wall of thug bastards.

They split apart and out walks the nasty fat piece of shit that transported me and the girls the day before. Only this time his face is bruised and his mouth missing a few blackened stubs.

"Delaney." I growl.

"Drop the knife," he sneers and chuckles when I do as he asks. I'm not stupid, you don't bring a knife to a gun fight. "You remember the Diablos, right? You killed a few top ranks in their crew."

"Couldn't have been top of shit if they were that easily killed." I shrug and he laughs, his gaping mouth on full display. *Fuck, he's gross.*

"I don't think they agree," he thumbs to the thugs over his shoulder. "Luckily for you, they want to kill your boys more than you, and so do I." He motions for them to grab me, and I laugh when all four of them step forward.

"What? You think I can't handle four men at the same time?" Their steps falter and I laugh maniacally, "alright, alright. Let's go," I walk forward towards an SUV. "But I ain't sitting with fatty."

They open the backend of the SUV and I roll my eyes. "Tie her up," the walrus calls out and I grin.

They grab my arms behind my back and tie my wrists, much like the driver dude did. Fuck, I never even got his name.

"Where are we going?" I ask, sounding bored, and hopping up into the back.

"To New York." Fatty answers as they slam the door shut.

At least we'll be back on home turf, and I know Blaze will figure this out. He'll know how to find me.

And when he does, he and I will make it rain red.

Acknowledgments

C.A. Rene

Rachael!!! We finished it and with minimal stress! Thank you for letting me rope you into a co-write because Selene and her boys are everything. Writing this series with you is so much fun and I can't wait until I have all these pretty books on my shelf.

To our Betas: Jocelyn, Maddy, Gemma, Alyssa, Lo, and Kristen. Thank you, ladies, for all your help with making our book baby as perfect as can be.

To Sammi!! Thank you for how hard you love this book and thank you for promoting it as hard as you do. I really appreciate every single thing you do for me and all my book babies. This cover?! So amazing and the interiors you put so much work into, you really are my Gryffindor Wizard. I love love love you.

To my ARC Team!! WE ARE BLACK SLAUGHTER!! You guys are hella dark bitches and I am here for it!! Thank you for finding me and loving the unconventional love stories I write. Strap in, it's only getting weirder.

Bloggers, Bookstagrammers, Booktok! I see you all and I am so grateful to each of you for the love you've been showing this series, Rach and I seriously appreciate it.

To our readers new and old, thank you so much for supporting us. Thank you to all the ones that read our novella in Violent Tendencies and asked for more, it was because of you that we continued the series!!

R.E. Bond

Only one more book to go! Can you believe it?

Massive shout out to my girl Chrissy for being the best co-writer in existence. I'd be so screwed without you, love you bunches!

To Sam from TalkNerdy2me, who's put up with so many apology messages because my dumbass forgot stuff. I'll send you more calming candles so you don't murder me, Love you!

Most importantly, to all the readers who have given this series a chance and have shared their love for it on social media or messaged either myself or Chrissy personally. Love you guys so, so, so, much and this wouldn't have happened without you guys!

About the Authors

C.A. Rene

C.A. Rene is married (but dreams of a RH of her own) with two kids (assholes) and lives in beautiful (cold most of the year) Toronto, Canada. To escape from life's pressures (more assholes) she brings fingers to keyboard and taps out her imagination. Most of the stories floating in her head contain blood, angst, and dark dark love.

Lover of all things dark. I love to read it, write it, own it, eat it, whatever it. My addictions include WINE, books, and coffee, in that order.

R.E. Bond

R.E. Bond is a dark romance author from Tasmania, Australia. She is obsessed with reverse harem books, especially if they have M/M! She collects paperbacks as a hobby, has read or written every day since she started high school, and constantly needs music in her daily life. She loves camping and rodeos in the summer, and not getting out of bed in the winter. Coffee and books are life, and curse words are just sentence enhancers.

Also by R.E. Bond

Watch Me Burn

Pretty Lies
Twisted Fate
Beautiful Deceit
Ignite Me
Perfectly Jaded
Don't Fear the Reaper

Reaped

The Reaper Incarnate
Claiming the Reaper
Hunting the Reaper

Anthologies

Violent Tendencies

Also by C.A. Rene

Whitsborough Chronicles

THROUGH THE PAIN
INTO DARKNESS
FINDING THE LIGHT
TO REDEMPTION

Whitsborough Progenies

IVY'S VENOM
CARMELO'S MALICE
SAXON'S DISTORTION

Desecrated Duet

DESECRATED FLESH
DESECRATED ESSENCE

Hail Mary Duet

BLUE 42
RED ZONE

Reaped

THE REAPER INCARNATE
CLAIMING THE REAPER
HUNTING THE REAPER

Sacrificial Lambs

SING ME A SONG
SONG OF TENEBRAE
A VERSE FOR CAELUM

Anthologies

VIOLENT TENDENCIES

DARKEST DESIRES

CPSIA information can be obtained
at www.ICGtesting.com
Printed in the USA
LVHW021051050522
717840LV00050B/2517